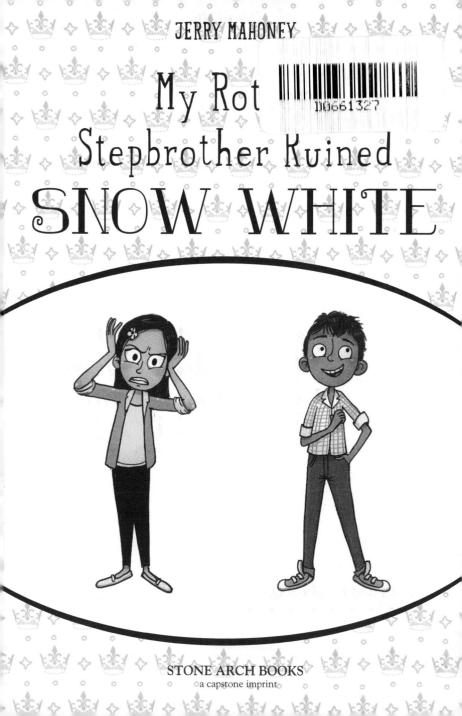

My Rotten Stepbrother Ruined Fairy Tales is published by
Stone Arch Books, A Capstone Imprint
1710 Roe Crest Drive
North Mankato, Minnesota 56003
www.mycapstone.com

Text © 2018 Jerry Mahoney
Illustrations © 2018 Stone Arch Books

Library of Congress Cataloging-in-Publication Data is available on the Library
of Congress website.

ISBN: 978 1 4965 4463 6 (library hardback)
ISBN: 978 1 4965 4467 4 (paperback)
ISBN: 978 1 4965 4479 7 (eBook PDF)

Summary:
Eleven-year-old Holden is visiting his dad in Germany and finds he can't
escape fairy tales wherever he goes. On a tour of Snow White's castle, the
story gets broken. Holden and his stepsister, Maddie, are transported to the
fairy tale world to fix the now karate-chopping dwarfs and triumphant Wicked
Queen. There he must decide if he wants to move to Germany to live with his
dad and leave his stepfamily forever.

Illustrations: Aleksei Bitskoff

Designer: Ashlee Suker

Printed in China.
010375F17

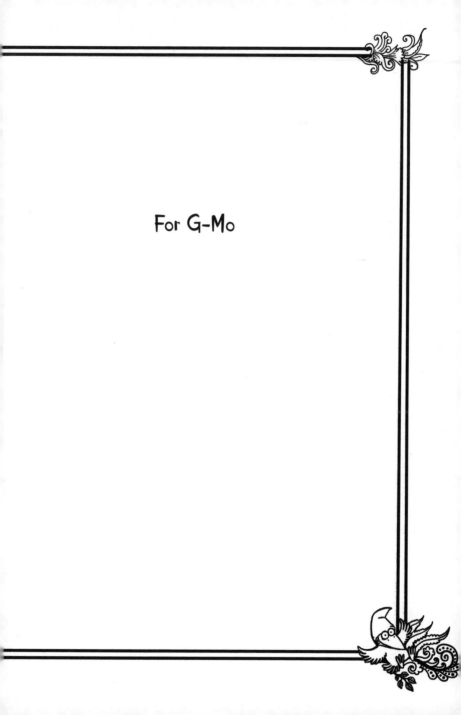

For G-Mo

Maddie stepped through the door of the tiny cottage and saw seven small beds, lined up side by side. There were seven teeny chairs around the dinner table, seven petite coat hooks on the back of the door, and seven shrimpy wardrobes filled with seven miniature mining hats and pocket-sized pickaxes. She twirled around in her beautiful dress, humming a happy song. It was a dream come true for her. She was Snow White, standing in the dwarfs' cottage!

"Maddie, they need you in makeup!" Mrs. Greenberg said.

"Be right there!" Maddie replied. It was the dress rehearsal of the school's production of *Snow White and the Seven Dwarfs*. It was also the first time Maddie had ever snagged the lead in a play. Good thing her friend Tasha wasn't jealous like the Wicked Queen, the part she was playing.

Maddie approached her stepmother, Carol, who had volunteered to do the makeup for the show. For the first time, Maddie got a glimpse at how Tasha was going to look in the scene where the Queen disguises herself as an old beggar woman. She barely recognized her friend, with her rotten teeth, crooked nose, and lumpy skin.

"What do you think, Snow White?" Carol asked Maddie. "Does she look wicked enough for you?"

"I want to go hide in the woods already," Maddie said. "Where'd you get all this makeup?"

"Well, they didn't have the budget for the professional stuff, so I improvised. The lumpy skin is just oatmeal. The rotten teeth come from chewing gum I dyed black. And the nose is papier mâché."

"Maddie, your stepmother is a crafting genius," Tasha said.

"I know," Maddie replied. She thought of all the cool things Carol had done for her, like making her Belle costume for Halloween or transforming their living room into a desert oasis for her *Aladdin*-themed birthday party. She'd helped build a beautiful set, too. Still, something about this production nagged at Maddie. "I was just thinking," she said. "Wouldn't it make sense if Snow White made herself ugly?"

"Huh?" Tasha said.

"Well, the Wicked Queen wants to kill her for being beautiful. But Snow White's not vain. She should just eat some fried food, let her skin break out. Then the queen would leave her alone, right?"

Tasha shrugged. "But that's not how the story goes."

Maddie couldn't stop herself, though. "And what happened to the huntsman? If he really wanted to help Snow White, shouldn't he have told the King what the Queen was trying to do? I mean, Snow White has a dad, right? I know my dad would notice if I ran away to live with seven strangers because my stepmom was trying to kill me."

"Well, I get a little annoyed when you don't clean your room," Carol said with a smile. "But I've never considered murder."

"Sorry," Maddie said. "I don't know why I keep thinking about these things."

"Maybe you miss your stepbrother after all," Carol replied. "He always had a lot to say about fairy tales."

"You do sound like him," Tasha agreed.

"Don't say that!" Maddie insisted. The very thought that she was becoming like Holden made her blood boil. He'd been gone for the last week, and it was pure bliss for her.

For his birthday, Carol got him a plane ticket so he could visit his dad in Germany. He wouldn't be back until after the show was done. Ugh, if he were here, he'd be going on nonstop about everything that was wrong with *Snow White*. Come to think of it, that probably was why Maddie kept obsessing over the plot holes herself.

"I do wish he could be here to see the show," Carol said.

Tasha nearly fell over at the thought. "Are you kidding?"

"Yeah, no offense," Maddie added. "I know he's your son. But he does not like fairy tales. Or plays."

Carol shook her head gently. "Well, he may not admit it, but I'm sure he'd enjoy seeing his stepsister as Snow White."

"No way!" Maddie assured her. She sat down in the makeup chair, and as Carol applied foundation to her face, she began to wonder what Holden was up to in Germany. He'd probably found a million new things to complain about.

Holden was literally holding on for his life. The uneasy grip of his arms around his dad's waist was the only thing keeping him from flying off the motorcycle and going splat on the Autobahn, a crazy German highway with no speed limit. They weaved between lanes, past weird European cars, as a majestic wooded valley unfolded below them, far down the side of a sharp, unforgiving cliff. Holden peeked around his dad's side just long enough to get a look at the speedometer. 110! Whoa!

Germany was awesome!

A few minutes later, they arrived at his dad's favorite spot: an outdoor restaurant. Tons of German people sat at long tables in a grove of trees, and the whole place smelled like pine and salty meats.

His dad took him to the counter to place their order, and Holden decided to play it cool. "*Guten Morgen*, my good man," he said to the cashier. "*Eine* chicken nuggets, *por favor.*"

The cashier broke out laughing. Holden's dad chuckled along with him. He spoke to the cashier in German to explain his son.

"What?" Holden asked. He could feel his face turning bright red.

"Well, let's see," his dad replied. "You said good morning, for starters, and it's 8 p.m. Then, you ordered chicken nuggets, and they only serve sausage. At least you were polite and said 'please,' although in Spanish."

"Guess my German is *nein* good."

His dad grabbed their food, then led him to a couple of open seats.

"I can't believe we were just going 110 miles an hour on your motorcycle!" Holden said.

His dad laughed again. "Probably because we weren't. They go by kilometers here."

"Oh," Holden said, disappointed.

"It's still pretty fast," his dad assured him.

Holden gazed around him. Strings of lights dangled from trees, twinkling like fairies. Just up the hill from where they were was a beautiful castle. It almost felt like . . . yuck, it almost felt like a fairy tale.

"What's wrong?" his dad asked him. "You're rolling your eyes."

"Just when I start to like this place, it reminds me of Maddie."

"Oh, right. She loves fairy tales, doesn't she?"

Holden nodded. "Her whole life is fairy tales." If only his dad knew just how true that was. He felt like he could tell his dad almost anything, but the one thing he couldn't share was how he and Maddie had been getting sucked into fairy tales lately.

All Holden had to do was point out the plot holes in one of Maddie's annoying stories, and then the two of them would get pulled into his tablet. Then, they'd become characters in the story and have to fix it so it still had a happily ever after. That was the only way they could get back home.

"Well, you know," his dad said, "this is the village where the Brothers Grimm grew up."

Holden groaned. "Of course it is! I can't escape fairy tales!"

"Definitely not here you can't. There's fairy tale junk all over this town." He pointed to the castle on the hill. "They say that castle is what inspired the Grimms to write *Snow White*. There's even a magic mirror inside. You can tour it if you want."

"Me?" Holden said. "No way. I hate fairy tales. They don't make any sense."

Holden's dad snickered. "Tell me about it. I mean, why did Snow White just wait around the dwarfs' cottage for the Queen to come kill her? Why didn't she train the dwarfs in karate or something? Seven dwarfs against one stuffy old Queen? They could've kicked her butt!"

Holden smiled. He had so much in common with his dad. They always had so much fun when they hung out. He wanted to tell him how he felt, but he didn't want to sound sappy. So what he said was, "Dad, I love Germany."

"Well," his dad said, "then you should move here."

Holden was so shocked he nearly spat out his sausage. "What?"

"Yeah, my company's transferring me here permanently. Maybe you can come live with me."

Holden checked his dad's face to make sure he was serious. This was huge. He never thought his trip to Germany might last forever.

"That would be . . ." Holden wasn't sure what to say.

"It'd be an adventure. Dude, we'd have so much fun. I'd enroll you in an American school, buy you some lederhosen."

"What's lederhosen?"

Holden's dad laughed. "They're these goofy German overalls. You'd look hilarious in them!"

"Maybe I'll skip the lederhosen. Other than that, though, I could get used to this place."

"Well, we'd have to talk your mom into it."

"Wow," Holden said, overwhelmed by the thought. Could he really see himself living in Germany? Could he really move away from his mom, his stepdad, and Maddie?

His dad walked to the cashier to order dessert, and Holden looked around him again. Germany was so cool, yet so different from Middle Grove, New Jersey.

Would he actually want to live here?

Chapter 2

Maddie was surprisingly calm on opening night. She had rehearsed so many times, she felt like nothing could go wrong. As the school auditorium filled up, she couldn't help peeking out at the crowd. There was her dad, sitting in the front row with two bouquets of flowers, one for her and one for Carol, who was busy putting the finishing touches on the cast's makeup.

Maddie felt bad for her dad having to sit all by himself. It would've been so satisfying to see Holden beside him, forced to watch a fairy tale without interrupting and pointing out the flaws.

Tasha was freaking out. "OMG, I can't remember my lines! Maddie, what am I going to do?"

"Just relax," Maddie told her. "We've rehearsed a million times. When you show up at my door, you say you're an old peddler woman selling apples."

"What?!" Tasha said. "I don't remember that scene at all!"

"How can you not remember that?" Maddie laughed. "It's the most famous scene in the story!"

"Oh, no!" Tasha whimpered. "I'm totally blanking!"

Before Maddie could calm Tasha down, Carol came jogging up to her. "There you are, Maddie!" she said. "I wanted to check this color for your acne in act two." She held a makeup tray up to Maddie's face.

"My what?" Maddie said. "Snow White doesn't have acne!"

Tasha gasped. "Now *you're* forgetting the play! This is a disaster!" Tasha ran back to the dressing room in a panic.

Carol shook her head. "I'm sure it'll all come back to you when the curtain rises," she said. "Everyone knows Snow White makes herself ugly to get the Wicked Queen off her back." Carol stuck a few fake zits on Maddie's face.

"What?" Maddie wondered. Did she hear that right?

"Not bad, if I say so myself!" Carol said, admiring her work. "You're ready to go!" She picked off the zits and hurried on to the next cast member. She didn't realize, but she left one pimple on Maddie's nose.

Maddie was in a daze. She had mentioned during rehearsals that Snow White should've made her skin break out. Was it possible that . . . ? No, only Holden could break the stories. Right? Or could it be that she'd done it herself this time?

"Hi-ya!" shouted Joey Katarka, who was playing one of the seven dwarfs.

Maddie wheeled around and saw the dwarfs attacking each other with kicks, punches, and yelps. "What are you doing?" she asked.

"We're preparing for the karate fights," Joey replied.

"In *Snow White*?!" Maddie said. She may have mentioned acne, but she never said anything about the dwarfs doing martial arts. That sounded like something Holden would come up with.

She wondered if he knew something about this.

"Five minutes to curtain, everyone!" Mrs. Greenberg shouted.

Maddie ran to check her copy of the script, nearly getting karate chopped by Ashley Lizander on the way. When she picked it up, she could see from the title alone that the story had gone through some pretty major changes: *Snow White and the Seven Butt-Kicking Dwarfs*.

Ugh, Holden! This had to be his doing — and, well, maybe a little bit hers, too. As she flipped through the script, she saw page after page of dialogue she didn't recognize, scenes that had never been part of the play before. Snow White getting acne; the huntsman confessing to the King! It was a totally different story. It was just like what happened with *Cinderella*, *Beauty and the Beast*, and *Aladdin*. All of a sudden, the fairy tale was broken. There was no more happily ever after. Worst of all, Maddie didn't know any of the lines anymore, and the curtain was about to go up.

"How long has the script been like this?" she asked around her.

"Only about a hundred and fifty years," Carol replied, as she pasted a beard onto a dwarf's chin nearby.

"Carol! Can I borrow your phone?" Maddie begged.

"But honey, the play's about to start."

"I need to call Holden!"

"Holden?" Carol seemed confused. "He— he called me earlier. Have you talked to him lately?"

"Not in a week," Maddie explained. "And he and I have something urgent to discuss. It can't wait another second."

Snow White Castle, gimme a break! Holden thought. With his dad at work, he decided to take a look at the town's tourist trap, the big castle up on the hill. It irked him to no end that he flew 4,000 miles away from his stepsister, only to find himself surrounded by fairy tale nonsense in a totally new place. Well, as long as he was here, he figured he might as well check it out, if only so he could make Maddie jealous. Maybe he'd take a few selfies with his tablet. That would drive her nuts.

Most of the signs Holden saw were in German, but it didn't matter. He was pretty sure they all just said a bunch of silly fairy tale junk. Stuff like: "This lame tree gave the Brothers Grimm the idea for the stinky poison apple." And "This statue of Snow White was put here because no one else wanted it." And "Go back to your hotel. This place is a waste of time."

Sure, a place like this might've impressed the Brothers Grimm in 5,000 BC or whenever they wrote their awful stories, Holden thought, but he and Maddie had actually been to the fairy tales, and this place was a tool shed compared to Cinderella's McMansion or the Beast's sweet pad.

On his way in, he passed by a gift shop and bought himself a sweatshirt with the name of the castle in German: Schneewittchen-Schloss. He loved thinking of how screamingly jealous Maddie would get when she saw him wearing it. He'd tell his friends it was German for *Skateboarding is not a crime*, so they'd think it was cool, too.

With his purchase in hand, Holden decided to skip the tour everyone else seemed to be going on. He just wanted to explore this place on his own, starting with the snack bar. He was in the mood for some good German chocolate. He picked up a map on the way in and tried to guess what the German word for *snack* was.

"*Toilette?*" Nope, that wasn't it, although he'd make note of that for later.

"*Ausfahrt?*" Probably not, but he'd have to find out what that meant, because it sounded hilarious.

"*Der Spiegel?*" Well, that started with an *s*, so it seemed like a good bet for snacks. He decided to head for *der Spiegel* and hope he smelled some primo strudel baking.

When he reached the top of a winding stone staircase, he found a sign pointing the way to *der Spiegel*. Finally! He was a little bummed out, because he didn't smell anything delicious baking, but he decided to keep heading in that direction anyway. The sign led him to a large room filled with old furniture. That was it. It wasn't an animatronic stage show or a 4-D immersive experience. *Der Spiegel*, if anything, must've been German for *boring room*.

Holden groaned. Why would they have signs pointing to this place? All it had were some ugly chairs, some creepy candles, and a mirror that was roped off for no good reason. At least he had his trusty tablet along, so he could check the e-book and see what the deal was. To his surprise, the tablet was already on, its screen was glowing, and the e-book for *Snow White* was already open.

This was not a good sign.

Sure enough, the title page looked totally different than it used to. "*Snow White and the Seven Butt-Kicking Dwarfs?*" Holden read. He couldn't help chuckling at the new title. "Awesome." As he flipped through, all the new illustrations showed just how much the story had changed. First Snow White was smearing oatmeal on her face for some weird reason. Then she was giving the dwarfs what looked like a karate class. Then the huntsman was in the dungeon with some strange-looking ladies. As Holden skimmed through the pages in shock, he heard a voice call out from behind him.

"Hey!" the voice shouted.

Holden jolted. He had thought he was alone in the room. "Who said that?" He looked around, but there was no one else there. Was he hearing things? He shrugged, then started to leave again.

"Over here!" the voice said.

Holden took another look, but still, he didn't see anyone. What was going on? Did they have hidden camera prank TV shows in Germany?

"Where?" he said.

"In *der Spiegel!*"

"What's that? I thought it was a snack bar."

"No! The mirror, snotface!" the voice replied.

Snotface? Holden gritted his teeth. That could only be coming from one annoying fairy. He gazed across the room and nearly leapt out of his skin. Sure enough, Resplenda's face was staring back at him from the mirror. She was the same fairy who had cursed Maddie and him. Because of her, every time he pointed out a flaw in a fairy tale, he and Maddie had to become characters in the story and fix it. "Boo!" she shouted.

"Great," Holden sighed. "Now you're bugging me in real life, too."

"Oh, boo-hoo. Poor you. I was going to tell you how to break the curse, but if I'm bothering you, then toodle-oodle-oodle!" She started to fade from the mirror.

"No, wait!" Holden rushed toward the mirror, wondering if there was a button he could press to bring her back.

"Oh, okay," Resplenda said, returning. "Second chance for a sassypants! Who's the nicest in the land? Me, me, me!"

"Yeah, you're a real peach," Holden said. "Tell me. Is there really a way I can break the curse? For good?"

"Oh, yes. The answer is simple and totally legal. To break the curse, break *der Spiegel!*"

"The mirror? That's it? I just have to break the mirror?" Holden said. "Done!" He picked up a chair and heaved it over his shoulder. He was about to swing it and smash the mirror, when Resplenda cowered in fear.

"WAIT!" she screamed. "Don't break the fake! This isn't the real magic mirror, you little flake!"

"Oh, come on!" Holden moaned as he put the chair down. "Are you telling me I have to go into the fairy tale to do it?"

"Oh, don't act like you haven't done this before!"

"But Maddie's back in New Jersey. How can I—?"

Holden felt a buzzing in his coat. He pulled out his tablet and saw he was getting a video call request from Maddie.

"You should probably answer that," Resplenda said. "Until then, smash, smash, see ya in a flash!"

With a quick burst of light, her face disappeared from the mirror.

Holden realized this was a great opportunity to make Maddie jealous. He quickly threw on the Schneewittchen-Schloss sweatshirt he'd just bought, then picked up the call. "Maddie? How funny you should call, when I'm standing here in Snow White's castle." As Maddie came into focus, he saw that she was dressed just like Snow White. "Whoa, are you already there?" he asked.

"What? Holden, I'm at the school play." She panned around behind her so he could see the backstage area.

"Oh, whew! I thought you were in the story!"

"Don't be too relieved," she said. "Somehow, this production of *Snow White* has seven karate-chopping dwarfs in it. I'm guessing you might know something about that?"

Holden laughed. "That was my dad's idea, actually. Hey, what's that on your face?"

Maddie looked at her image on the phone and saw the zit Carol forgot to remove.

"Oh, nothing." She pulled it off.

"I never said anything about Snow White's face being zitty city!" Holden said.

"Okay, so maybe I made a few comments about the story, too."

Holden cracked up. "So you're criticizing your own stories now? Classic!"

The stage manager walked behind Maddie. "Two minutes to curtain!"

"Holden, what are we going to do?" Maddie whispered into Carol's phone. "I don't know the lines to *Snow White and the Seven Butt-Kicking Dwarfs*!"

"Well, I'd love to help, but I'm on vacation," Holden said.

Just then, the mirror lit up behind him, and Resplenda appeared. "Snotface!"

Holden turned away so Maddie wouldn't see the mirror. "Okay, fine. Let's go fix this fairy tale."

"Great. Let's both pull up the *Snow White* e-book." Maddie opened Carol's books app.

"Places, everyone!" the stage manager shouted. Maddie began to panic as her castmates scrambled onto the stage behind her.

"Is this even going to work?" Holden asked. "We're in different places, you're on a phone. This isn't like we normally do it."

Maddie sighed. "Well, we have to try. You know what to do," Maddie said. "On the count of three . . ."

They both put their hands on their screens. "One, two, three . . ." Then, in unison, they said, "Once upon a time . . ."

Holden faded into his tablet screen just as a tour group reached the mirror room. As for Maddie, everyone in the cast was so busy getting into place that they didn't notice her being swept off her feet and into the screen of Carol's phone.

In two different parts of the world, the two stepsiblings disappeared at exactly the same moment.

Chapter 3

For the first time in a week, Maddie and Holden were together in the same place. Of course, where they were was nowhere. It was the blank page of a book, the gateway to the magical world of fairy tales. Everything was totally white except for the two of them, reunited against an empty background.

Before they could even say hello to each other, words began to fly above their heads. *Trees, wildlife, wooded path, forest.* This was how the story took shape.

By now, Maddie and Holden were used to this. Maddie was brimming with anticipation to find out what character she would be. In *Beauty and the Beast*, she got to be Belle! Then again, in *Aladdin*, she got stuck as a camel and a monkey. Would she end up as the Wicked Queen – or as one of the dwarfs? Ugh, what if she had to go through the story as the poison apple? She just hoped that she could at least be a human.

Holden saw the words *bow* and *arrow*, and the next thing he knew, he was holding them. This was already turning out to be cool for him. When the background finished filling in, Maddie and Holden found themselves in a clearing in a forest. The word *huntsman* settled over Holden's head. Maddie was still wearing the same dress from her school play. The name *Snow White* dissolved above her.

Maddie pumped her fist in excitement. Score!

"What's the bow and arrow for?" Holden asked. "Do I get to slay a dragon or something?"

"No, you're the huntsman. The Queen ordered you to kill me."

"Look, I know we don't get along sometimes," Holden said. "But I don't think I could really—"

"Thanks," Maddie interrupted. "I wasn't suggesting you actually do it. The Queen ordered you to, but the huntsman doesn't have the heart to go through with it."

"Oh, right," Holden replied. "Hey, what's this?" He pulled at a handle on his waist and unsheathed a dagger. "Whoa, cool! This huntsman really came prepared."

"Holden, put that away before you hurt yourself!" Maddie scolded.

"What? So I don't get to use the hunting gear at all?"

Nearby, they heard the sound of snorting. A wild pig rustled through the bushes, sniffing for food.

"No, you do," Maddie said, "but on him." She pointed to the pig. "You cut out his heart and tell the Wicked Queen that it's mine."

Holden looked sadly at the pig as it sniffed around for food. "Aw, what did he do? How about I just go back and waste your stepmom instead?" He mimed firing a few arrows. "Pew! Pew! Pew! I mean, she totally has it coming, right?"

"You could never defeat her. She knows dark magic, remember?"

Holden shook his head. "Well, I'm not slicing up some innocent pig. This is your twisted fairy tale, not mine. You do it!"

He handed Maddie the dagger, but she immediately backed away.

"I can't hurt a pig!" She sighed. "You're right. We'll have to find some other way for you to convince the Queen that you killed me."

Holden jumped up on a tree stump in excitement. "I've got it! We'll paint a big rock to look like your head, then I'll shove it in a box and wrap it up like a present. The Queen will open it up and go, 'Aah! Aah! A head! It's so gross!'"

Maddie rolled her eyes. "How are we going to get a rock that—"

"Wait! Better idea!" Holden interrupted. "We find someone who looks exactly like you, who's about to die of natural causes. No, we forge a death certificate using — no!" Holden was leaping all around.

Maddie had seen him get this way before, and she knew the best thing to do was to let him burn out all his excess energy until he got distracted by something completely unrelated.

"How about a phony funeral? Closed casket!" Holden exclaimed. "No! I dress up like her magic mirror and tell her— No! No! No! Ooh, puffer mushroom!"

There it was. Holden saw a large fungus growing on the side of a tree and forgot what he had been talking about. Finally, he stopped shouting ridiculous ideas. "Okay, let's figure this out," Maddie said, thinking aloud, while Holden poked at the mushroom with an arrow.

"I love these things!" Holden giggled. He continued jabbing the puffy mushroom, sending a mist of spores shooting out of it.

"Wait! That's it!" Maddie said. "We can take a mushroom and make it look like a heart!"

"Oh! Good thinking! And then we stage a fake funeral with a girl who looks just like you—"

"I think the heart will be enough," Maddie said, pulling a fist-sized puffer mushroom from a tree trunk.

"I don't know," Holden said, eyeing the mushroom. "It doesn't look much like a heart."

"Not yet," Maddie said. "But I've learned a thing or two about crafting from your mom. I have some ideas." Maddie darted into the forest and began scavenging for things that could help her turn a pale brown mushroom into a veiny red heart.

Chapter 4

Holden took a look at the red, twisty lump Maddie was holding in her hands. It was totally disgusting — and so realistic he almost expected it to start beating.

"Cool!" he said. "How did you make it?"

"First, I soaked some rose petals in creek water to make a red dye. Then I found some twigs, stripped off the bark, and slid them just under the mushroom's cap so they'd look like veins bulging out. Then I took pine needles and—"

Holden rolled his eyes. "Okay, fine, you're a genius. Crafting is even more boring than fairy tales." He grabbed the fake heart from her and tossed it into a satchel he wore over his shoulder. "Now, I'll deliver it to the Queen, and you get the dwarfs ready to kung fu the juice out of her."

"But how can I teach them karate if I don't know it?"

"Oh, come on. You've seen karate movies, haven't you?" Holden said.

"A couple." Maddie shrugged.

"Well, that's how I learned," Holden replied. "I'm pretty much a black belt now."

"Holden, karate is an ancient art that's been developed by skilled masters over the course of thousands of years. You can't just—"

Before Maddie could finish her thought, Holden jumped back and forth, karate chopping like a maniac. "Kiai! Kiai! Kiai!" he shouted. It didn't look anything like in the movies. It was more like a crazy person swatting at a bee. "See? It's easy. You try it."

"Okay," Maddie sighed. She jumped and swiped with her arms, making grunting sounds as she did. "Unh! Unh! Unh!" Then, she decided to go for a high kick. She reared back and threw her entire body into it, snapping her foot up so high that her shoe flew off into some bushes.

"Enhhh!" she grunted, as she lost her balance and tumbled onto her butt.

"What was that?" Holden said.

"You didn't like my moves?" Maddie stood up, rubbing her sore butt with her hand.

"No, the moves were fine," Holden assured her. "But you're totally blowing it on the most important part of all!"

"The focus?" Maddie guessed. "Keeping my eye on my opponent?"

"Your yell!" Holden corrected. "Everyone knows the key to any karate fight is having the best yell."

"Really? Are you sure that's—?"

"Um, you've only seen two karate movies," Holden said. "I've seen, like, five. So trust me. Now, let's work on it. Come at me like you're opening up a can of whoop-butt!"

Maddie took a deep breath, then karate chopped in Holden's direction. "Unh!" she grunted.

"That sounded like you were opening a can of tuna fish. Let's try this. Think of something that makes you mad," Holden said.

"Okay, I can do that."

Maddie concentrated really hard and tried to remember a time when she'd been especially angry. There was the time she missed watching the Olympics figure skating finals because Holden was hogging the TV playing video games. Then, she thought of when he reset her Instagram password to *holdenrulz*. Then, she thought about *Cinderella*, *Beauty and the Beast*, and *Aladdin*. Man, he was such a creep in *Aladdin*!

There was something that made her mad, all right, and she was staring right at him.

"KEE-YAAAAH!" she thundered. She charged toward Holden full force, snarling like a bull. She was so fierce that Holden ducked out of the way, and Maddie ended up karate chopping a tree. Her arm sliced through two branches and knocked them both cleanly off the trunk.

Holden gave her a pat on the back, impressed. "Whoa, not bad! What were you thinking of?"

Maddie tried to think fast. "Um . . . spiders." As much as Holden drove her nuts, she didn't have the heart to tell him that the sight of him made her mutilate a tree.

"All right then. You're ready to teach some dwarfs to kick butt. And I'm ready to give a Queen her stepdaughter's heart in a bag. *Sayonara*, sucka!"

"*Sayonara*, sucka?" Maddie repeated.

"Yeah, it's how they say goodbye in karate movies. Trust me. You gotta use that line."

Maddie rolled her eyes. Why did she ever take Holden's advice about anything?

Chapter 5

The moment Maddie split up from Holden, it began to get dark. It got very dark, very fast. Soon, she found herself in a section of the forest that was much creepier, and no matter which way she turned, she only seemed to be going further into its depths. The moon cast an eerie glow over the woods. The shadows of the long, jagged, leafless branches looked like pitchforks ready to poke her if she slowed down. It reminded her of the Dark Forest in *Beauty and the Beast*, only this time she was alone, and there was no magic entrance to the fairy world in sight.

She tried to assure herself that she simply had an overactive imagination. She thought of when she was a little girl and her father read her a scary story at bedtime. "It's just a story," he'd remind her. "Nothing can hurt you."

Of course, that advice was totally useless here. This was a story, too, but she wasn't just reading it. She was living in it. If the soreness of her butt from her karate fail was any indication, things in this story could most definitely hurt her.

She kept following the path, hoping to reach the dwarfs' cottage so she'd be safe at last. Nearby, she heard a wolf howling at the moon. A moment later, there was a rustling in the bushes. Then, on the other side of her, more rustling. Slowly, shadows emerged — first in front, then behind her. She stopped cold, as wolves crept out onto the path, more and more of them, until there were so many she couldn't count them. She had never been so terrified in her life. The wolves closed in on her — fierce, determined. She had to think fast.

She remembered what Holden had taught her about picturing your enemy's face. She looked around at the feral creatures preparing to pounce on her, and she tried to imagine Holden's head on each of their bodies. There they were, dozens of Holden heads on dozens of wolf bodies, their fangs dripping with drool. Though it was just in her mind, she could visualize them all trying to ruin various fairy tales for her, in Holden's whiny voice.

"Hansel and Gretel would've thrown up from all that candy!" she envisioned one of the wolves saying.

"Little Red Riding Hood's grandma must've awfully hairy if she confused her with a wolf!"

"Why didn't Rapunzel just cut her hair?"

"KEE-YAAAAH!" Maddie's fear became fury, and she let loose a deafening yell. As she did so, she began karate chopping with both arms at once. "YAH! YAH! EEE! HAH! HAY! HO!" She kicked her legs in every direction. She was so scared, she closed her eyes, but she never stopped making a commotion. In all her life, she had never yelled so loudly before.

The wolves were baffled. None of Maddie's moves actually hit any of them, but she kept flailing robustly and making so much noise that they weren't sure how to react. This girl was crazy!

Maddie couldn't believe they hadn't attacked her yet, so she cautiously opened her eyes to see what they were doing. To her amazement, the wolves were retreating, feeling that this lunatic human was not worth the effort. They disappeared back into the bushes, leaving the path ahead clear for Maddie to resume walking.

Maddie smiled, relieved but also impressed with herself. *Wow*, she thought. *I must be really good at karate.*

Chapter 6

Holden knew when he had reached the Wicked Queen's palace, because it looked surprisingly similar to the Snow White palace he had visited in Germany, with two big differences. One, it was much bigger and better built, and two, there was no place to buy tickets. It was a real palace, with no signs directing tourists where to go and, from what he could gather, no clear way inside either.

It was at the very top of a hillside, and the cobblestone path that led up to it dead-ended at a wall. There had to be a hundred windows, but he didn't see a single door. He stood at the base of the massive structure and shrugged. Did the fairy tale architect forget to build a way in?

As he tried to figure out what to do, he felt a dark shadow fall over him. A chilly wind swept past, causing him to shudder. "Well?" a voice hissed. "Do you have it?"

Holden turned to discover a tall, pale woman towering over him. She was beautiful and terrifying all at once, in a dark cape and with a sparkling crown on her head, enc

long, wavy black hair. She kind of looked like his old gym

teacher, the one who showed no mercy during dodgeball.

"Whoa, way to sneak up on a guy!" he said. "I just killed your stepdaughter, you know? You could at least say 'hi.'"

"Give it to me!" she demanded, extending her long, bony fingers toward his satchel. "Give me her heart!"

"Okay, fine. Chill out. Here's the lousy heart." Holden unfastened his satchel, and the Wicked Queen eagerly snatched up the fake heart inside.

Holden gritted his teeth while she inspected what he knew was just a painted mushroom.

The Wicked Queen stared closely at the heart as she turned it over and over in her hand. "I would've thought that little do-gooder would've had a much bigger heart."

"Oh, ha ha," Holden said. "Nope, normal size."

With a wave of her arm, the Wicked Queen made a doorway appear on the side of the castle. Holding the fake heart close to her chest, she walked inside.

Holden was stunned at the magic display, so stunned that he stood there just wondering what to do.

"Well, come on!" the Wicked Queen ordered him.

Holden scurried after her inside. "Right, thanks."

"You have done well," the Wicked Queen told him as he caught up to her.

"Thanks," Holden said. "I'll be honest. It was my first royal murder. I was a little nervous."

The Queen led Holden through the corridors of her castle. He was awed how much larger and more opulent it was than the one in Germany. High ceilings with glimmering chandeliers the size of swimming pools. Polished stone floors. Grand winding staircases leading to the upper floors and turrets. "Now this is a castle!" he said.

The Queen stopped dead in her tracks. "Why are you acting as if you've never been here before? You've worked for me for years."

Uh oh. Holden had to think fast. "It's just, everything was always about Snow White. Snow White this, Snow White that. Now that she's gone, I can finally notice how pretty everything else around here is." The Queen stared down at Holden, as if waiting for him to say something. It took him a moment to realize what she must be after. "Like you, of course, Your, um, Prettiness."

The Queen smiled. "My name is Nefaria."

"Okay, Your Nefaria-ness."

"You flatter me," she cooed. Then, she resumed walking.

Holden couldn't help being freaked out by how calm she was about all of this. She had just had her stepdaughter killed, or at least so she thought. Didn't she at least feel a little guilt?

He thought about how close his mom had become with his stepsister. It annoyed him sometimes, but isn't that how it was supposed to be? None of this jealousy and killing nonsense. Poor Snow White came from one messed-up blended family.

He had no idea how to solve the royal family's problems, but one thing he could take care of was his rumbling belly. "You know, I could really go for a good meal right now. Slicing up a princess's body parts really took a lot out of me."

"For your service to me, you will be handsomely rewarded," the Queen said, continuing to march down the hall. "But first . . ."

She opened the door to a large room full of old furniture. It didn't seem like anything special, yet for some reason it looked strangely familiar to Holden. Was it possible he had been in a room just like this once before? Then, he saw something that told him exactly where he was.

"*Der Spiegel!*" Holden shouted. He was gazing at his own reflection in the wicked stepmother's magic mirror!

"This mirror will be able to tell me if my stepdaughter is really dead," the Wicked Queen said. "Or if I need to have *you* killed instead!"

Holden swallowed hard. He and Maddie came up with a pretty good plan, but they never thought about what the magic mirror would tell the Queen. If it spilled the beans, he was dead meat.

44

Chapter
7

Maddie's adrenaline was still racing as she reached a clearing in the forest. There, she found an adorable little cottage sending puffs of smoke skyward from its chimney. It was very small, with a doorway that only came up to her shoulders at its highest point. In case there was any doubt where she was, she spied a stable in the yard with seven miniature ponies inside.

Finally, she could relax. She'd made it to the dwarfs' cottage without becoming wolf food. She shuffled up a cobblestone path to the front door and gave a gentle knock. "Hello? Anyone home?"

There was no reply, so Maddie knocked a little louder. "Hello?" Well, at least one thing stayed the same from the story. The dwarfs were probably hard at work in the mines. She knew that Snow White was supposed to open the door and go in, but it just felt so rude. Then again, it's not like she had much choice. If she stayed outside, she'd be prey for wolves and wicked stepmothers. Plus, she was exhausted. She'd just been through a long hike and fought off a pack of wild animals. She'd totally earned the right to kick back and crash for a little while.

When she squeezed through the miniature doorway, there were no dwarfs inside. Pretty much the only thing she saw was dirt. There were dirty dishes everywhere, dirty clothes, and, most of all, dirty clumps of dirt. Dirt was propped into little mounds under the carpet, it was streaked in muddy footprints across the floor. There was even dirt hanging from the ceiling! How could such tiny guys even reach that high?

Maddie couldn't believe how messy this place was. It was almost as bad as Holden's room! She knew Snow White was supposed to be a neat freak who tidied up this rotten stinkhole before the dwarfs got home from work, but she didn't have it in her. She hated cleaning.

Besides, she had a more important mission right now: making herself ugly. Otherwise, the Wicked Queen would see her image in her magic mirror and know she was still alive. Then, she'd come looking for her, and who knows what she'd do to Holden, her huntsman.

She remembered how Carol made Snow White look ugly in the school play. Thankfully, there was plenty of old food among the dishes stacked up in the sink. She even found some weeks-old oatmeal, which she slapped onto her face to make her complexion look bad. Then, she took some soot from the fireplace and used it to blacken her teeth. Carol had really taught her well.

Maddie checked a mirror and saw she'd done a pretty good job of tarnishing Snow White's beauty. Still, something was missing.

Then she remembered back to when she was in *Beauty and the Beast*. One day, she left her cottage straight after waking up, with a bad case of morning face and bedhead. Of course! That would really top off this look. Even better, it gave her an excuse to put off cleaning and take a nap.

She tried squeezing into one of the dwarfs' beds, but there just wasn't enough room. Her long legs dangled off the edge, and she couldn't get comfortable. Then, she got an idea. No one bed was her size, but if she pushed a few of them together, she'd have room to stretch out across them.

She quickly put three of the beds together, end to end. She tried to add a fourth one, but when she moved it, the entire bed toppled over. At first she thought it was her fault, but when she looked down to inspect the bed, she saw that two of the legs were broken. She felt bad for whichever dwarf had been sleeping on that one.

It turned out three beds was plenty. She laid back across them and had just enough room to stretch out. As soon as she laid down, she felt her eyelids get heavy, and before she breathed three more breaths, she was sound asleep.

Chapter 8

Holden wondered if they used guillotines in Germany. He'd never heard of any headless Germans, so he was probably safe. Unless, of course, they used some even more barbaric type of execution in this country, like strangling prisoners with lederhosen or drowning them in German chocolate. One way or another, the Wicked Queen was sure to torment him if *der Spiegel* blabbed that Snow White was still alive.

His only hope was to change the subject — and fast. He jumped in front of the Queen before she could reach her mirror, hoping to distract her. "So, let me get this straight. You're going to talk to a mirror about whether I killed Snow White? What's next? Are you going to ask the sofa what's for dinner?"

The Queen narrowed her eyes at her huntsman. "My mirror is magic," she explained. "It knows everything, and I will ask it what I always ask it — who is the fairest in the land. If you've truly done as you've said, it shall tell me that I am, not that dreadful stepdaughter of mine."

"Hold on. You mean you have a magic mirror that can answer all your questions, and the only thing you ever ask it is whether you're the fairest in the land? What about asking it what matters most in life? Or why food that's good for you tastes so bad, while food that's bad for you tastes so good? Or how porcupines hug without poking each other full of holes? Am I right?"

"Stop your foolishness!" she said, swatting him aside. "I need to face my mirror." Holden swallowed nervously as she began to turn toward the magic mirror. "But first!" she said, "I must make sure I look my best."

Pivoting away from the mirror, she sat down at a vanity and began brushing her hair. *Wow,* Holden thought. *She's so vain she won't even look in the mirror until she knows she's at her most beautiful. This lady is completely cray-cray.*

Wait — the mirror! Of course! Resplenda told him that if he smashed the mirror, the spell she placed on Maddie and him would be broken. Then he wouldn't have to worry about guillotines or wicked queens or any of this nonsense anymore.

That settled it. He wasn't going to wait for the Queen to talk to the mirror. He was going to take action — and this was the perfect opportunity. While she fixed herself up, he was going to find something he could use to break glass.

He quietly gazed around the room. What could he possibly grab? All the furniture was so big and heavy-looking. There was a marble statue of the Queen, but there was no way he'd be able to lift that. There were fancy bowls and glasses, but they were all displayed in cabinets behind thick layers of glass. Before he could use them to shatter the mirror, he'd have to find something to shatter the glass so he could get to them. That would never work.

Thankfully, the Queen was so wrapped up in what she was doing that she didn't see Holden plotting. She continued brushing her hair, over and over. There was something strange about the way she did it. No matter what part of her head she was trying to reach, she never adjusted or removed her crown. It certainly wasn't easy for her to brush her hair with her crown on.

Her crown! Wait. That was it!

The crown could break the mirror. All he'd do is grab it, then hurl it before Nefaria could react. He was just inches away from it. He could do this, he told himself. At the very least, he had to try. His heart pounding in his chest, he began to reach his hands up . . .

And just then, the Queen turned and looked at him. "There! You have to admit I look stunningly beautiful, right?"

Holden quickly pulled his arms back so she wouldn't see what he was doing. He was so nervous he could barely speak. "You look okay," he said. "But I think you missed a spot."

"I did?" Nefaria replied. She gently touched her hair with her hands, looking for any strand that might be out of place. It was a challenge to do her hair without looking in the mirror, but she clearly had a lot of practice at it. "I don't feel anything unusual."

"Right on top," Holden said, breathing heavily from fear. "U-u-under the crown."

"Oh, no!" Queen Nefaria replied. "I simply can't reposition my—"

"Here, I'll get it!" Holden said, ignoring her. He lunged forward and swiped the crown off the Queen's head. He felt so bold. He did it!

Then, the Queen began to scream. "AAAAAAH! What are you doing?"

Before Holden could throw the crown at the mirror, he froze. The crown hovered in front of him, hanging in midair, and he was unable to move it.

"What happened?" he asked.

Then, he noticed something even stranger. Dangling from the crown as it hung suspended near his hands was hair. The Queen's long, gorgeous black hair. It was floating there, still attached to the crown.

"No one touches my crown!" Nefaria hissed. She stood with her arm extended, a finger pointing at the crown. Holden remembered she had dark magic powers, which she must be using to hold the jewel-encrusted headpiece in place.

"Huh?" Holden said, and as he turned toward the Queen, this strange sight began to make sense.

To his amazement, the Queen was completely bald. Her head was smooth and hairless and perfectly egg-shaped. If there wasn't a face on it, a chef might try to crack it and make an omelet.

"How dare you!" Nefaria thundered. Using her magic, she pulled the crown and the wig back and placed them on her head. Thankfully, she was too worried about getting them on straight to lash out at Holden. "You fool! It takes me an hour to get my hair looking just right."

"I'm sorry," Holden said. "I didn't know you were—"

"What? That I was what?!" she asked him. It was clear she wanted him to forget he ever witnessed her secret.

"Um, nothing. Just beautiful, as usual."

Queen Nefaria stomped across the room, her hands clutching her hair to her scalp to keep it from falling off. Before she left the room, she turned to spit one final furious message at Holden. "We'll have our talk with the mirror later."

Holden breathed a sigh of relief as he watched her disappear into the hallway, then, feeling bold, he called after her, "Don't forget you owe me a feast!"

Chapter 9

When the short, rounded door to the tiny cottage creaked open, the seven stout men who entered were not surprised to find their home a shambles. That, they were used to. Among the seven of them, not one of them had any interest in keeping things tidy.

What did surprise them, as they stepped inside their house after a long day's work, was the sound of a woman's voice coming from their beds.

"Rotten stepbrother . . . wolves . . . rotten Holden . . . ," it muttered.

Quietly, the dwarfs crept across the room and surrounded the beds, which they were startled to find had been pushed together so that this strange woman could lay across them.

The seven men gathered quietly to size up the stranger. As they bent over her, they were shocked to see that her face was a filthy, blemished mess. Her hair was dirty and knotted.

A stream of snot dripped from her nose. As they examined her, the dwarfs uttered seven bewildered statements, one after the other.

"Who is she?"

"Is she a giant?"

"No, we're just small."

"Is she the princess?"

"No, the princess is beautiful."

"Maybe she's the Wicked Queen!"

"Yes, the Wicked Queen! The Queen who is wicked! That's who she is, and we must get her before she gets us! Hurry, hurry, hurry! On the count of seven!"

The woman continued to mumble and drool through her deep slumber. "Left me in the woods . . . karate chopping . . ."

The dwarfs shared a look and nodded in agreement that they must pounce on this stranger and tie her up before she hurt them.

"One . . ."

"Two . . ."

That was as far as they got, when their counting caused the strange woman to stir in bed. She rolled over, stretched, and let out a mighty, garbling yawn. It startled the dwarfs so much that instead of counting off his number, the next dwarf yelled, "Grab her! Now!"

Maddie jolted from sleep as seven small men jumped on her all at once. "Ow! Hey!" she screamed. The dwarfs were frantically trying to pin her down. They twisted and yanked, struggling to subdue her. Every time she broke free from one dwarf's grip, she was sieged upon by six more. It was no use. Maddie was going to have to try something more drastic to fight them off.

"KIAIIIIII!" she wailed, karate chopping with both arms at once. When she looked around at the dwarfs, she saw them as seven mini Holdens, all sneering at her. She leapt to her feet and began kicking in their direction. At once, the dwarfs backed off, springing off the beds and scurrying to take refuge behind chairs and bookcases.

From their safe places, the dwarfs shared a confused look. They weren't sure what was going on, but they all seemed to agree on one thing: their uninvited houseguest was as loony as a cuckoo bird. They were all so shaken up, it took all seven of them just to ask one simple question.

"Wh-wh—"

"Who . . ."

". . . ah-ah—"

". . . are . . ."

". . . y-y-y—"

". . . you . . ."

". . . lady?"

Maddie stepped down off the beds to answer, but the last dwarf had more to say and he said it very quickly. "Because I think I speak for all seven of us when I say we're really confused. There are seven men who live here, no women, and you're a woman, so you can't be us, so you must be you and we don't know who that is."

Maddie approached the dwarfs gently. She wanted to be careful, because she probably really frightened them by being so fierce with her karate moves. "Yeah, sorry I had to scare you like that. I'm Snow White."

"I told you!" one of the dwarfs shouted.

"No, I told you!" said another.

"You told him!"

"He told him!"

"We told each other!"

"Who told you?"

The chatty dwarf stepped to the front and addressed his brothers. "It doesn't matter who told who, because nobody told anybody what they should've told somebody which was that everybody overreacted when we thought she was you-know-who."

The dwarfs all nodded in agreement, though Maddie seemed a bit confused by what he just said.

"Well, thank you," Maddie replied. "Don't worry. I don't want to hurt you. I really should've cleaned up when I barged in, but I was a little wiped out from being in a fairy tale and everything. I'll get to it, okay? I just had to escape my wicked stepmother. She sent her huntsman into the woods to kill me."

The dwarfs let out a collective gasp, seven times as loud as any Maddie had heard before.

"I know, right?" Maddie said. "She wants to be the prettiest woman in the land. That's why I made myself unattractive, so she wouldn't be jealous of me."

The dwarfs circled around Maddie, consolingly.

"You poor thing!"

"You can stay here!"

"We'll hide you!"

"We won't let her hurt you!"

"We love visitors!"

"Do you know how to cook?"

Lastly, the chatty dwarf patted Maddie on the shoulder. "We're good helpers, and you need help, so we'll help you, and if you can help out around the house, that would be helpful, too. In the meantime, help yourself to anything you like, like food. And like my brother asked, can you cook? Because that would be a big help."

"Um. I can make sandwiches and microwave pizza pockets," Maddie said. "But I'm guessing you don't have a microwave or even know what that is. Anyway, I'm not really supposed to cook unless my parents are home. But thanks for letting me stay here, um . . . you guys." She scanned their faces and felt bad that she didn't know any of their names. "If I'm going to be your houseguest, I'd should probably get to know you."

The chattiest dwarf smiled and bowed. "Happy to introduce ourselves, and nice to meet you, and we hope in return that it's nice for us to be met. Our parents wanted to make it easy on people, so they gave us each a name that started with a different letter of the alphabet. Now, to make it easy on you, we'll speak as we always do, in ABC order. Here goes!" He pointed to his first brother, and one by one, the dwarfs stepped forward and told her their names.

"I'm Abe!"

"I'm Bud!"

"I'm Cal!"

"You can call me Don."

"Edd here!"

"My name's Fox!"

The chatty dwarf took a deep breath. "And I'm Gustavo-Humberto-Ignacio-Jerome-Kevin-Lawrence-Michelangelo-Nicholas-Owen-Phillippe-Quentin-Richard-Steven-Thomas-Ulysses-Vernon-Wendall-Xavier-Yadad-Zachary."

Having finished his name, he sat down to catch his breath.

"How about I call you Gus?" Maddie said.

"Oh, that's much easier!" the dwarfs agreed.

"You're a genius!" Gus agreed. "I've wasted half my life saying my name. So . . . you want to start sweeping or doing the dishes, maybe a little laundry?"

Maddie looked around the cottage. It desperately needed to be cleaned, but the thought filled her with such dread. It was exactly like she felt whenever her dad asked her to clean her room. She knew the job needed to be done, but she just couldn't bear to do it at that moment. So she did what she always did in those situations . . . stalled.

"I have a better idea," Maddie told the dwarfs. "How about a karate lesson?"

The dwarfs all took a step backward. They shared another glance, thinking once again that this strange woman standing before them was most likely cuckoo banana pants.

Chapter 10

"Well, that was weird."

Holden stood before Nefaria's magic mirror, still thinking about the Wicked Queen's shiny, hairless head. No wonder she was so hung up on her looks. She'd spent her life covering up a secret from the world. He almost felt bad for her, but then he remembered she tried to kill her stepdaughter. Yeah, hair or no hair, she was still pretty awful.

It took Holden a minute to realize that being alone with the mirror gave him the golden opportunity he'd been hoping for: to smash it and break the spell. Once again, he looked around the room for something that could shatter the glass. Then, he realized it was probably easiest just to use the huntsman's big boots to kick it until it broke. Nice! He was actually going to get to do some karate of his own.

"*Sayonara, Spiegel!*" he said, pulling his foot back. He swiftly thrust it in front of him and was just about to hit the glass, when he heard a familiar voice again.

"WAAAAAAIT!" it screamed.

"WHA—?!" Holden startled, twisting his body to avoid kicking the mirror. The move threw off his balance and knocked him off his feet. He tumbled to the floor with a thud, landing on his knees. "Ow!"

As he looked up from the floor, he saw Resplenda gazing down at him from the mirror. "Ouch, ouch, a bump for the grouch!" she taunted.

"Why did you do that?"

Resplenda giggled. "Well, for one thing, I wanted to make you fall down! Hee-hee! On your knees!"

Holden rolled his eyes and pulled himself back onto his feet.

"Oh, you're asking for a smashing!" He pulled off his boot and got ready to shatter the mirror with it.

"Oh no, no, no! That's not how the story's supposed to go!" Resplenda shook her head.

"You said I could break the window to get out of this nightmare."

"Yes, yes, but the story's a mess. Snow White's in hiding, and the Queen's plan's a success. If you break the spell, the story stays broken as well!"

Holden thought for a moment, then shrugged. "Eh, what do I care?"

"You may not care, but I think you know someone who does." Resplenda's face faded from the mirror and up came an image of Maddie and the seven dwarfs. They were standing outside their cottage, and Maddie was showing them some karate moves.

Holden smiled. "She's really teaching them karate!" He had to admit, it was pretty cool that he'd added some smooth martial arts moves to this boring tale. Well, maybe *smooth* was the wrong word. He watched as one of the dwarfs tried to replicate the karate kick Maddie just did, but he toppled over and landed on his side. "Ha!" Holden laughed. "It *is* funny when people fall down."

Resplenda's face reappeared in the mirror. "She stuck to the deal. She did her thing. Now you told her you'd talk to the King!"

Holden sighed. He hated to admit it, but this insufferably rhyming fairy who cursed him was right. He made a promise to his stepsister, and he should at least try to keep it. Besides, if he left the story now, Queen Nefaria would be the hero of it. What kind of moral would that leave readers with?

'If somebody's prettier than you, have them killed?' Even he couldn't let little kids go on thinking that.

"Fine, I'll talk to the King!" he pouted. "Just a quick chat. 'Dude, your wife's a murderer, gotta go.' Then I'm breaking you into a million pieces."

"Oh, huntsman!" an evil voice called.

"Whoa, ho ho! Better go! Toodle-oodle-oodle!" Resplenda disappeared from the mirror just as the door swung open and Queen Nefaria stepped inside.

"Dinnertime already?" Holden asked.

The Queen stepped into the room. She had fixed her hair and the crown. "Dinner will have to wait. The King has returned."

"Oh yeah?" Holden said. He was a little bummed, as this probably meant no feast. The Queen wasn't likely to reward him for ratting her out as they carted her off to the dungeon. But if that was the way it had to be, he'd just grab some pizza pockets out of the fridge when he got home.

The Queen hung her head, pretending to be sad. "My poor, dear husband. He's going to be so upset when he hears about his beloved Snow White's untimely passing."

"You mean you haven't told him yet?"

"Well, you were the only witness. I figured you should tell him."

"What?" Holden said. "You want me to tell the King that I— that I killed his daughter?"

Two armed guards appeared beside the queen. She pointed at Holden, and they marched up and grabbed him. "You can tell him that she was attacked by wolves. That you tried to save her but couldn't."

"You want me to lie to the King?"

The Queen smiled. "Well, we don't want to get you in any trouble, do we?"

Chapter 11

The dwarfs did not pick up on karate as easily as Maddie hoped. The first time she put two of them together to spar, all they could do was giggle uncontrollably and say, "You start!"

"No, you start!"

When Abe punched his brother Don ever-so-gently in the arm, he felt so guilty that he ran back inside the cottage in shame and slammed the door behind him. And when Edd raised his foot to kick, he toppled over and landed face-first on a tree stump. There, he sat and whimpered until Maddie finally gave him a kiss to heal his boo-boo.

Maddie was about to give up hope. The dwarfs were simply too kind and peaceful to become the kick-butt fighting machines she would need them to be in order to take on the Queen.

Then, one of the dwarfs who'd been sitting quietly stood up and cleared his throat.

"Might I have a turn?" he asked meekly.

"Sure, Bud," Maddie shrugged. "If someone will agree to fight you."

Only one of the others seemed interested in the task. Cal shrugged and quietly held up his hand to volunteer.

"I guess if no one else wants to, I'll give it a shot," he said.

"All right then," Maddie replied. "On the count of three." She could barely muster the energy for the countdown at this point. This showdown was sure to be as anticlimactic as all the others. "One . . . two . . . th—"

"KEEEEE-YAH!" Bud screamed, before Maddie had even finished saying *three*. He then unleashed a volley of karate chops all over his brother's tiny body.

"UNH! UNH! UNH!" Cal grunted in return, delivering one swift roundhouse kick after another near Bud's face.

Maddie backed away from their mini melee, not wanting to get caught in the middle. "Whoa!" she said. "What's going on?"

"Those two fight a lot," Abe explained with a shrug. None of the dwarfs seemed the least bit surprised to see Bud and Cal's dust-up.

"Fix my hat rack!" Bud squealed as he chopped Cal in the arm.

"Fix my bed!" Cal replied as he kicked Bud in the leg.

"No, you fix my hat rack!"

"No, you fix my bed!"

It went back and forth like this, as the brothers kicked, chopped, and blocked with abandon.

"What are they arguing about?" Maddie asked.

"Cal broke Bud's hat rack," Abe explained, "so Bud broke Cal's bed."

Maddie remembered the bed that fell apart when she tried to slide it over. "Oh, whew. I thought I broke it."

Bud and Cal continued to attack each other. "KA-OOH!" Cal shouted, running up the side of a tree and doing a backflip over his brother's head.

"Wha-OOF!" Bud roared, as he rammed his fist against that tree, snapping clean through the trunk. The tree began to wobble and fall right toward Cal. Everyone gasped. Cal ducked out of the way just as the tree thudded to the ground with such force the whole forest seemed to shake.

"I'll get you for that!" Cal wailed. He started kicking another tree trunk in an attempt to knock it over. "Unh!"

Maddie was horrified at how viciously they fought. At the same time, though, she was kind of excited. Maybe these guys could take on the Queen after all.

Chapter 12

When it came to big, important speeches, Holden usually liked to wing it. It was how he got through the toast he gave at his mom's wedding to Greg, and he ended up dishing out some really sweet zingers off the top of his head.

"I compared notes with your daughter," he said with a wink to Greg, "and you're a lot more generous with allowance than my mom, so now that we're family, I want to be on your payroll."

He got a big laugh from the crowd on that line, and an even bigger laugh when he followed up with, "No, I'm serious!"

Classic.

Then again, he probably would've done better on his oral report on World War II if he had planned what he wanted to say first.

He only got one sentence out before the teacher said, "You haven't prepared for this, have you?"

Just because he started with, "So . . . World War II was, like, kinda, the sequel to World War I. You know, bigger, more expensive, but not nearly as good."

One thing was for sure. He was going to tell the King the truth, the whole truth. And man, was it a doozy! His wife hired a huntsman to kill his daughter. Now the daughter was hiding in the woods in a house full of seven dudes. It was almost like one of those crazy talk shows his mom sometimes watched, where long-lost family members showed up to reveal shocking secrets in front of a stunned studio audience — live!

He'd overheard her watching those shows plenty of times, so he had a pretty good idea how they'd present a story like this.

"You thought your wife was loyal, but you're about to find out about a shameful betrayal she committed right under your nose! Then later, in a stunning twist, she'll come face-to-face with the stepdaughter she thought she'd murdered, here to tell her amazing tale of survival!"

That would make the King fall right off his throne. "Wha—?!" he'd say, spitting out the contents of his royal goblet.

As cool as that sounded, maybe it would be better to soften the blow. Be a little more formal about it. Something like this: "Your Highness, I'm sorry to be the one to have to tell you this, but all is not well in your fine kingdom." Then he'd give a nice dramatic pause before lowering the boom.

Then again, maybe simple was best: "Dude, you've been hosed. Your wife is a screwy nut waffle."

No matter which way he chose to say it, the Queen was sure to go crazy. She'd probably raise her fist at him, vowing revenge as guards dragged her kicking and screaming off to the dungeon.

At least that part would be kind of fun.

Soon enough, the guards threw open two enormous jewel-encrusted doors. Trumpets blared, and Holden followed the Queen down a long red carpet toward the King.

"My dear Nefaria!" the King said, as he laid eyes on the Queen. He rose from his throne and kissed the back of her hand. "How I missed you on my travels!"

"And I, you, my eternal love!" the Queen replied. Holden couldn't help rolling his eyes. She was such a phony.

The King looked around, peering over the Queen's shoulders.

"I called for my daughter, Snow White, as well. Why have you brought me the huntsman instead?"

The Queen lowered her head. "I'm afraid the huntsman has some most unsettling news for you," she said, with a nod to Holden. "Please, huntsman. Tell His Majesty what happened when you took Snow White to the woods."

The King looked at Holden, who still hadn't decided which approach to take with this news. The King seemed like a nice guy to him, and Holden didn't want to upset this dude. He decided to stall. "Okay, well, it was really wild. It's going to be kind of shocking, like, so . . . do you maybe want to sit down for this?"

"HE KILLED HER!" The Queen's voice bellowed at maximum volume.

"Wha—?!" Holden shouted.

The Queen extended a finger accusingly at Holden and narrowed her evil eyes at him. "It was cold-blooded murder! She had no idea it was coming. Our poor daughter!" Her voice quivered as she spoke. She pretended like she was holding back tears.

"Wha—?!" the King sputtered.

"It's true!" the Queen screeched. "Murderer! Murderer!"

The King began to weep. "No! No! Not my dear daughter!"

This was totally not going as Holden had hoped. On the one hand, he had to admit, the Queen was a really good actress. On the other, he needed to explain himself, fast. "No!" Holden insisted. "I didn't! She's— she's lying!"

"If I'm lying, then how come he brought me this?" The Queen held out her arm, and one of the guards handed her the huntsman's satchel.

"Uh oh!" Holden said, as the Queen handed it over to the King. "This is not going to look good."

"What is this?" the King asked.

"Don't open that," Holden said. "Please."

As Holden stood there speechless, the Queen flipped open the satchel for the King to see. "It's Snow White's heart! He kept it as a token of his cruelty and brought it to me to show off!"

The Queen yanked the heart from the satchel and held it aloft for everyone in the room to see. Even the normally stone-faced guards gasped.

"Whoa!" one of them said.

"This is a dark day for our kingdom!" another agreed.

"B-b-b-b-but . . . it's not what you think!" Holden begged, stammering. He had never in his life felt so many people giving him such hateful glares.

The King rose to his throne, furious. "You foul monster!" he roared. "Guards, seize him!"

In an instant, the King's soldiers surrounded Holden and grabbed him firmly by the arms. The last thing Holden saw as they encircled him was the Queen smirking with delight at his capture. "She set me up!" Holden yelled, but it was too late. The King couldn't hear him over the clamor of the guards' marching feet.

"Take him to the dungeon! Immediately!"

The Queen patted her husband's back, consolingly. "I'm as devastated as you are," she lied.

As the guards dragged Holden from the room, all that could be heard was the muffled sound of his cries for mercy. "She's a screwy nut waffle!" his fading voice called out.

Chapter
13

Maddie was amazed at how much stamina Bud and Cal had. They'd been fighting for nearly an hour and showed no signs of letting up. At this point, the tussle had been going on for so long that the two brothers seemed to be running out of valid complaints, and as a result, their insults were getting weirder and weirder.

"You smell like potatoes!" Bud shouted at his brother.

"You sound like a goose!" Cal retorted.

Listening to them, Maddie couldn't help wondering if this was how she sounded when she fought with Holden. No wonder her parents got so annoyed when they argued.

"Wow," Maddie marveled to the other dwarfs, who were all watching helplessly. "They really don't like each other."

"Oh no," Abe disagreed. "They're best friends!"

"Best friends?" Maddie repeated. "They haven't said one nice thing to each other."

"Sometimes people show their friendship in strange ways," Edd said.

How could you be best friends with someone when you fought constantly? Maddie wondered. It didn't seem to make sense.

"Uh, guys," she said, stepping closer to where the two dwarfs were wrestling on the ground. "You really showed you know how to fight. You can stop now."

"Never!" Cal said. "Not until he says he's sorry!"

"You say you're sorry!" Bud replied.

"No, *you* say it, goose voice!"

And just like that, the fight was back in full force. Maddie bent over and tried to pry them apart with her hands. "Come on, stop it!" she said. Neither of the dwarfs listened to her, and she didn't have the strength to separate them. "You guys!"

Maddie gave up. There was nothing she could do. So much for her plans of fighting the Queen. Most of the dwarfs were too peaceful, and the two who weren't would never have any energy left when the time came. It didn't look like this story would ever get fixed.

Through all the squabbling, Maddie heard the sound of a horse approaching. It clopped through the woods over trees and branches, heading toward them with urgency. As the horse rode up to where they were, a man pulled on its reins and brought it to a stop right beside Cal and Bud.

"Whoa!" the man said. He hopped down off the horse and stepped into the fray. "What is happening here?"

"She made them fight!" Abe accused, pointing a finger at Maddie.

"Hey!" Maddie said.

"Well, stop it at once!" the man insisted, bending over the dwarfs.

"No! He's a dodo bird!" Bud said.

"He's a stinkyface!" Cal replied.

"I said, stop!" the man declared. With firm, muscled arms, he picked up the two dwarfs and pulled them apart, holding them separate from each other off the ground, just out of each other's reach. They tried for a moment to swipe at each other, but seeing it was no use, they soon gave up.

"Wow, he's strong!" Abe marveled.

"And handsome!" added Edd.

Maddie took a look at the man. Edd was right. He looked like a movie star — or, better, like Jake Templeton, the cutest boy in school. His teeth were perfectly straight and perfectly white. Not a single hair was out of place. His blue eyes sparkled in the sun. He was dressed neatly in a crisply pressed military outfit, full of medals.

"Who are you?" Bud asked, dangling from the man's arm.

"I'm Prince Rodrigo of Encantadoria. I often come to these woods to ride my horse." Now that Bud and Cal had calmed down, he placed them back on the ground. "As for you two, I want you both to say something nice about each other."

"Never!" the dwarfs replied, in unison.

"Come on, now! The way you both shouted 'Never!' at the same time makes me think you have a lot in common. Surely, you have something nice to say."

"Well, he is really good at mining," Bud shrugged.

"Aw, only because you taught me the best way to hold the axe," Cal replied.

"Brother!" Bud said, spreading his arms wide for a hug.

"Brother!" Cal replied. He ran into his brother's embrace, and the two of them held on tightly, best friends once again.

"Wow, you're really good at that," Maddie complimented the Prince.

"Thanks. I have a lot of practice keeping peace in my kingdom. So tell me, why did you ask those two men to fight?" the Prince asked her.

"I just wanted to train them," Maddie explained. "We have to fight the Queen . . ."

"Queen Nefaria?" Prince Rodrigo asked. "Why are you fighting her?"

"It's a long story," Maddie said.

"She tried to have Snow White killed!" Edd explained.

The Prince took another look at Maddie and smiled. "Snow White! Of course! I should've known that's who you were. You're even more beautiful than they say."

Maddie smiled, then remembered how awful she actually looked, with her bed hair and morning face. "I think you might need glasses," she joked.

The prince shook his head. "I like that you didn't spend hours getting made up. It allows your natural beauty to shine through."

He smiled at Maddie, and she had to look away, because she didn't want him to see her blushing. This man was so sensitive, so understanding. When she was Belle in *Beauty and the Beast*, she went on a date with a man who was only interested in her outer beauty. She had to spend hours getting ready before seeing him, just so she'd look nice enough. Prince Rodrigo wasn't shallow, that was for sure.

"Why would Queen Nefaria try to kill you?" he asked. "Isn't she your mother?"

"Stepmother," Maddie corrected. "And she didn't personally try to kill me. She hired her huntsman to do it for her."

"But family is everything," the Prince replied. "Why would a woman want her own stepdaughter dead?"

Maddie sighed. "She's jealous of my beauty. That's why I gave myself morning face and came here to hide out."

"This is horrible!" the Prince replied. "I must help you work this out."

"Work this out? How could I work things out with her when she tried to kill me?"

"I believe everyone deserves a second chance, if you have it in your heart to give her one. Please, come with me, and I'll help you talk to her."

Maddie sighed. She knew this story too well. The Queen was evil, wicked. There was no hope for her. Still, the Prince was nice and he was offering a free ride to the castle. She motioned her hands toward the dwarfs. "Okay, but only if my friends can come, too."

"No problem," Abe said. "We'll follow along on our ponies! Come on, guys!"

The dwarfs all scrambled to their barn to retrieve their ponies. All except Bud, who stayed behind, looking glum. "Cal fed my pony some bad oats, and now he has a tummy ache," he griped.

Up ahead, Cal stopped and turned around, angrily. "Oh, yeah? Well, you know what Bud did to me?"

Before the exchange got any more heated, Prince Rodrigo stepped in between the men. "Maybe you two could ride together."

Bud and Cal looked at each other and smiled. "Fun!" they both cheered.

Maddie breathed a sigh of relief. "Wow," she said, as Prince Rodrigo helped her onto his horse. "You really are good at making peace."

Chapter 14

Holden could feel the air getting colder and mustier as guards led him downstairs to the palace dungeon. It reminded him of the descent to Cinderella's dungeon, a creepy, forbidding chamber of doom. He could only imagine the horrors he'd see when they opened the door. Torture devices? Rats scavenging for food? Would his fellow prisoners be frightening brutes like Cinderella's barbarian cellmate?

"Well, hi there!" called a cheerful voice as soon as Holden stepped inside the dungeon.

"Huh?" Holden said, getting his first glimpse of his new surroundings.

"Howdy-do!" said another perky voice.

Dungeon didn't seem to be a fitting word to describe this place. It was bright and sunny, with no bars, no rats, and no torture devices. The prisoners were all women — four of them — and they were strolling back and forth, sipping tea, and taking nibbles of food from neatly arranged platters. Not only did the room not seem very prison-like, but the inmates didn't seem very criminal either. They were polite, friendly ladies. It was less like prison and more like one of those PTA meetings his mom would sometimes host.

"Am I in the right place?" Holden asked.

The prisoners chuckled. "Yes, this is the dungeon," a lady with very dirty, dusty skin replied. "Welcome, welcome! I'm Gracie, and who might you be?"

"I'm a very confused huntsman right now," Holden admitted.

Gracie smiled. "Probably not what you were expecting, I guess. Well, that's because we have the best guards who take such good care of us." She nudged one of the guards playfully in the arm.

"Well, we have the best prisoners to take care of," the guard gushed in response.

"No, you're the best!" the lady said, giggling.

"You're the best!" the guard chuckled.

"What's going on?" Holden asked. "Where are the barbarians and traitors and thieves? Did any of you try to overthrow the King?"

"Oh, no!" the women laughed.

"These nice ladies would never do anything like that," the guard explained.

"Then why are you in a dungeon?"

The women all hung their heads, sadly. For the first time, their smiles faded.

The guard stepped forward. "I'll say it. The Queen locked them up for being too pretty."

The other guard nodded in agreement. "She wants to be the most beautiful woman in the land, so any time she finds someone prettier than she is, she puts them in the dungeon. She takes away their beauty products, deprives them of sunlight, won't let them take baths."

"Wait," Holden said. "So she puts you here to make you less pretty?"

"That's right," Gracie answered. "That's why I'm so dirty. It's why Lily's hair is so tangled, why Sakiya's teeth are so rotten." One of the women standing behind Gracie smiled, showing a mouthful of cruddy brown teeth.

"Yikes!" Holden said. "I mean, no offense. Other than that, you all look pretty nice. How did she get so obsessed with being beautiful?"

"She wasn't always like that," said the fourth woman, who until then had been silent. She stepped forward out of the shadows, revealing that she was covered all over with thick, tired wrinkles. "My name is Vivian, and I've known her since we were schoolgirls."

"But you're so much older than she is," Holden said.

"I'm 37!" Vivian retorted. Holden gasped, because that's how old his mom was. It was old, for sure, but not nearly as old as this woman looked.

Vivian put her hand on Holden's shoulder and began to share her memories of the Queen. "She was always so shy as a young girl. Insecure about her looks. I never quite knew why. Her parents certainly didn't help. They told her she was ugly and that she'd never get married. The Prince was the first person who ever complimented her beauty. When he became King, he asked her to be his Queen. I was the maid of honor at their wedding. She overheard him tell me how nice I looked in my dress. It was an innocent remark, but it made her furious with rage. Her first official act as Queen was to have me locked in this dungeon."

"We all have stories like that," Lily added. "Even after the wedding, she was always afraid the King would find someone more beautiful and leave her. The one thing none of us can figure out is why she's so unsure about her looks."

"I know why!" Holden said. "She's bald! With an egg-shaped head!"

The women all gasped. "No!" Gracie said.

"Yes! I took her crown off, and a whole head of hair came with it! You could've dyed her scalp pink and hidden it for Easter!"

Gracie shook her head. "And her parents never told her she was still beautiful."

Holden tried to take this in. He definitely thought the Queen looked odd without her hair, but maybe that's just because he wasn't used to seeing bald women. If she walked around proudly with her bald head exposed, maybe she could rock that look. It was certainly a better plan than locking all these good people in a dungeon.

"Now we're afraid for Snow White," Lily said. "She's grown into such a gorgeous young woman. We fear what the Queen will do to her."

The guard pointed at Holden. "She had him kill her!"

Again, the women gasped. "I didn't do it!" Holden said. "I took her to the woods and set her free. I have to get out of here so I can help bring her back. I need to tell the King what really happened."

The women shook their heads. "The King has no idea any of this is going on. He thinks she's still the same, sweet woman he married."

"Well, we have to tell him!" Holden said. "Ladies, let's get to work!"

Chapter 15

Queen Nefaria stood before her magic mirror, as she had so many times before. Something felt different this time, though. This time, she already knew the answer to the question she wanted to ask. Snow White was dead. Her other competitors were locked away in the dungeon. There was no doubt. She was the fairest in the land. So why did she still feel the need to talk to her mirror at all?

Was it possible that being the prettiest woman in the kingdom wasn't enough to make her happy?

No, of course not. How ridiculous. As she stared at her reflection in the mirror, she was struck by her own beauty. Her perfect cheekbones. Her silky skin. Her bright green eyes. Even her hair had everyone fooled. She had everything she ever wanted. All she could do was hope her husband never found out what she had to do to get it.

She thought back to what the huntsman said. Maybe there were other questions she should be asking her mirror.

Now that she'd settled the matter of her beauty, she decided to give one of them a try.

"Mirror, mirror . . . ," she said.

In an instant, Resplenda appeared, looking annoyed at being summoned. "You again? Look, you're fair, fair, fair! So there! Now, off I go to anywhere!" Resplenda started to fade from view.

"Wait!" the Queen said. "I have a new question!"

With renewed interest, Resplenda's image returned. "Ooh, ooh, ooh, something new! Ask me now, and I'll answer true!"

The Queen took a deep breath. What was it the huntsman had told her to ask? Besides the question about porcupines? Oh, yes. Now she remembered. "Tell me, Mirror. What is it that matters most in life?"

"Ooh, good query, my deary!" Resplenda said. "Wanna hear-y my theory?"

The Queen nervously shook her head. "Never mind. It's beauty, obviously. Beauty's the most important, and I have it. Thank you, Mirror!" The Queen turned around to leave.

"Hey, hey, hey, don't go away!" Resplenda said. Reluctantly, the Queen stopped. "Beauty's nice, but it comes with a price. If you really want to know the score, there are a thousand things that matter more."

"A thousand things more important than beauty?" the Queen said, in shock. "Name one!"

"Okay. Cookies!"

"Cookies?"

"They're number 872, but still, they outrank beauty. Except the ones with raisins. Nobody likes those. Only a rookie puts raisins in a cookie!"

"Just tell me the most important. Get on with it!"

Resplenda shook her head. "Creaky, crikey. You won't likey!"

"Please, tell me what it is."

"Husbands, daughters, mothers, sons. In all the world, family is number one!"

"Family?" the Queen spat. She sneered at Resplenda, turning angrily on her heels.

"You don't like family?" Resplenda asked. "I even like my Aunt Fantasma, and she has pickle breath!"

"My family was wicked!" the Queen hissed. "My father never said a nice thing about me. My mother called me Rat Face. I loathe my family!"

As she stormed across the room, Resplenda called out to her. "What about this family?" she said. She faded from the mirror, and in her place, there appeared a portrait of the Queen with the King and Snow White. They smiled warmly, arms around each other, in happier times. The Queen took one look at it and froze, guiltily.

"Hi-de-hoo, they're your family, too! And they've always been nothing but nice to you," Resplenda added.

The Queen sighed. Resplenda's words stung. Yes, she had a terrible family growing up, but she hadn't treated her own family any better. She lied to her husband and murdered her stepdaughter. "Well, that settles it. If family is the most important, then I need to have the best family in the land."

Resplenda returned to the face of the mirror and groaned. This lady was totally missing the point. "Bing-bing, bong-bong! Lady, you're totally, madly—"

The Queen shook her head dismissively. "Just show me! Stop the rhyming and the silly talk and show me who has the best family in all the land!"

Resplenda rolled her eyes. "Why does everyone hate my rhymes? It's more fun than how you talk!" Resplenda stuck her tongue out, then faded from the mirror. In her place appeared images of the seven dwarfs. There were scenes of them singing, dancing, and playing games, always bright and always jolly.

"Them?" the Queen hissed. "They're dwarfs!"

"It's not the size of the body that matters. It's the size of the heart! And each of theirs is seven times as big as yours."

The next image that came up was of Bud and Cal engaged in a heated karate showdown. "Hold on!" the Queen said. "They're fighting! That can't be the best family!"

"Even the best families fight sometimes," Resplenda said. "But they always forgive. And they never hire huntsmen to kill each other, if you know what I mean."

The Queen looked away, because she didn't want to catch a glimpse of her reflection at that moment. But out of the corner of her eye, she saw something in the mirror that didn't seem to fit with the rest of the image. Something light blue and red that fluttered in the breeze.

Resplenda returned to the mirror. "Well, if there are no other questions, I have a lot of people to curse, and I should get back to it. Toodle-oodle-oodle!"

"Hold on," the Queen said. "Show me that last image again. Where the little men were fighting."

Resplenda shrugged. "Sure. Whatever." She faded and put up the image of the dwarfs again. This time, a woman stepped in between the two fighting men and tried to break them up. She was wearing a blue and red dress.

"No!" the Queen said. "It can't be!"

As the Queen watched in shock, the woman's face was revealed, and indeed, it was just as the Queen feared. It was Snow White.

"She's still alive?!" the Queen shouted. "Snow White is alive!"

Resplenda giggled nervously, as the Queen scowled at her. "Uh . . . is that a question for me?"

Chapter 16

Despite all the time she had spent in fairy tales, Maddie hadn't grown the least bit bored with taking in the scenery. Every sight was like a sketch from a storybook, full of color, beauty, and life.

She felt a rush of wind through her hair as Prince Rodrigo's horse galloped through the kingdom's lush country hillsides. Behind them, the seven dwarfs rode on six ponies, following neatly in a line that stretched down a delicately winding dirt path.

"This is almost like a dream," Maddie found herself saying. Prince Rodrigo turned around, and she realized how funny that must've sounded. "I mean, it's my kingdom. I see it all the time. No big deal."

"I know what you mean," Rodrigo replied. "The world is so full of beauty. I only wish someone was painting everything we see and putting the pictures in a book to preserve them."

"Oh, they are," Maddie assured him, before catching herself. "I mean, in a way they are. At least, I like to think so."

"Well, a book about this horse ride with you," Rodrigo replied, "is one I'd never grow tired of reading."

Maddie blushed, and from behind her, she overheard the dwarfs commenting on the Prince's manners.

"Wow, he's so nice!" Abe said.

"He's very sweet," Bud added.

"I'd say he's thoughtful," Cal contributed.

"I declare him kind," Don tossed out.

"I still say handsome," Edd chimed in.

"To me, the word for him is *courteous*," Fox admitted.

"Those are six good words to describe him," Gus agreed, "but I have one great word which means all six of yours and so much more. One word for a thousand compliments, and that word is . . . *charming*. Furthermore—"

"Charming?" Maddie interrupted. She didn't hear anything else Gus said as he continued babbling. She just kept hearing the word *charming* over and over in her head. Of course. Rodrigo was Prince Charming!

Until that moment, she hadn't even thought about the love story in *Snow White*. Normally, after Snow White bit the apple, she fell into a deep sleep. The dwarfs thought she would never wake up. Then, along came Prince Charming, who fell in love with her on sight. His kiss brought her back to life. It was one of the most romantic moments in all of fairy tales. It was . . .

Kind of creepy, now that she thought about it.

Maddie had never seen it that way before, but since she was in Snow White's shoes, she wondered what it would be like to have a stranger kiss her while she was sound asleep. What if she woke up and found some unknown man hovering over her, claiming that he'd fallen in love with her while she was passed out cold? It wouldn't matter how handsome or charming he was. She'd think he was a bit odd. She'd definitely want him to back off, at least until she could get to know him better.

It was better this way, she realized. This altered story was giving her the opportunity to get to know Prince Rodrigo before he planted a smooch on her. He was cool so far, but she had no idea whether Snow White was supposed to end up with him.

When she and Holden went into *Aladdin*, it turned out that Nazeerah didn't need to marry Aladdin to be happy.

Maybe romance was in Snow White's future, maybe not. For now, though, the priority was fixing this mess with the Wicked Queen.

Soon, Rodrigo's horse led them into the dark woods. Maddie felt herself clutching the Prince's waist a little tighter as the sky turned gray and the crooked trunks of burned-out trees bent over the narrow path on which they rode. As disturbed as Maddie was, though, the dwarfs were even more freaked out.

"I don't like this place!" Abe said.

"It's making me uncomfortable!" Bud agreed.

"It's so dark!" Cal added.

"I think it's creepy!" Don nodded.

In the distance, Maddie could hear a rustling sound. All their chatting was attracting some unwanted attention. "Shh!" she scolded the dwarfs, but they were too wrapped up in their conversation to hear her.

"I have goosebumps!" Edd shivered.

"I have chills!" Fox continued.

Now, Maddie could see furry tails winding through the brush nearby. Sinister eyes glared at them from between the leaves. "I mean it!" Maddie said. "Quiet!"

This time, the dwarfs heard her, and they quickly stopped talking. Or at least, almost all of them did.

"She makes a good point," Gus said. "The best predators also have the best hearing, so our discussion sounds like their dinner bell. Our monologue is their menu. Consider this food for thought, or before we know it we could be food for—"

"Wolves!" Maddie shouted. As the dwarfs watched in terror, a pack of wolves stepped in front of them on the path, blocking their way. Rodrigo stopped his horse, and in an instant, they were surrounded by wolves, snarling and drooling, quickly closing in on them.

Rodrigo nervously caught his breath. "Fear not," he said. "I will handle this." He hopped down from his horse and bravely unsheathed his sword.

"Nah, it's okay. I got this," Maddie said. She leaped down beside him and took a karate stance.

"Hi-yah!" she shouted. She kicked as high as she could, first with one foot, then with the other. "AY! UNH!" Then she karate-chopped and punched the air. "WHOO! FA! OOS!" She turned to the dwarfs. "C'mon, guys. Back me up. You can do it!"

The dwarfs stepped up beside her and joined in, all of them doing any karate moves they could. "KEE-YAH! EE-YOH! WHOOWHOOWHOO!"

The wolves made the same confused expression they did the last time Maddie practiced her cuckoo karate on them, and this time, Prince Rodrigo looked just as baffled. The wolves looked to him, hoping for an explanation, but all he could do was shrug at Maddie's bizarre behavior.

"Yeah, taste the pain!" Maddie shouted, as the wolves backed away from her and the seven karate-chopping little men. "This is just a sample of what Snow White is serving up! KYAH!"

Prince Rodrigo began to smile, impressed at how Maddie's fighting, bizarre as it was, was working to repel the wolves. Soon, all of them scurried off into the woods, and the humans were alone on the dirt path, safe and sound.

"*Sayonara*, suckas!" Maddie cracked at the fleeing wolves. She filled with pride. Holden was right. It did feel good to say that line.

"Wow, that was—" Prince Rodrigo wasn't sure how to finish his statement.

"Yeah, I know," Maddie said proudly. She ran past all the dwarfs, high-fiving each one. "Nice work, guys! We are totally ready to fight the Queen!"

Rodrigo helped Maddie back onto his horse, patting his sword with one hand. "I might keep my sword handy, just in case."

Chapter 17

Holden was having a surprisingly fun time in the dungeon. The ladies loved to play cards, and they enjoyed all the cool games he taught them, like Go Fish, Chase the Ace, and Nutty 9s, which was a game he made up himself that was a lot like Crazy 8s, except you had to shout "Boo-yah!" and do a dance whenever you used a wild card.

Who would've guessed spending time with four grown-up ladies could be so much fun? He even started to think he might ask his mom if he could join in the next time she had her friends over to play Bridge.

Nah, probably not.

"Okay, ladies," Holden said, while he shuffled the deck. "This game is called 'Slap the 7s' and here is how it's played."

Before he could go into the rules, the door to the dungeon flew open, and in burst Queen Nefaria. "You didn't kill her?" she thundered.

Holden groaned and rolled his eyes, half because the Queen was angry and half because she interrupted their card game. "Of course I did. Why would you say that?" he asked.

Nefaria threw the satchel down in front of him, then opened it up to reveal the phony heart.

"Uh oh," Holden said, under his breath.

"I should've looked closer at this," Nefaria hissed, picking up the fake. She reached underneath the mushroom cap and pulled out some of the items Maddie had crafted to make it look real. "Hearts don't have pine needles in them! And these veins are just twigs, dyed red! This isn't a heart. It's a puffer mushroom!"

"Ridiculous!" Holden lied, but to demonstrate the point, the Queen hurled the object to the floor and stomped on it. Instantly, a thick cloud of spores rose up. Holden knew he was busted. "Fine. Want me to tell you how we dyed the twigs red?"

"How dare you defy my orders!" the Queen raged.

"Okay, you got me!" Holden said, trying to make light of the situation. "As long as we're getting everything out in the open, can we talk about how unfair you've been to these nice women? Locking them up for being pretty?"

Nefaria gazed at the prisoners. She was shocked to see Sakiya's teeth and Gracie's dirty skin. "These are the same women I—?" She stopped short, as her eyes settled on Vivian, once the maid of honor at her wedding. Though her skin looked old and wrinkled, the Queen recognized her instantly. "Vivian!" She was obviously shocked at how Vivian had changed during her time in the dungeon. "What's happened to your beauty?" she asked.

"I still feel pretty on the inside," Vivian replied, squaring up her shoulders with confidence. "How do you feel?"

The Queen turned to Lily and ran her fingers sadly through Lily's knotted tresses. "And you! You had such lovely hair!"

"You thought you could hide your problems by locking them away," Holden said, "but look what you've done to them."

As the Queen scanned their faces, Holden could see she was moved. "I've done horrible things," she confessed in a whisper.

"Yes," Holden agreed. "This is all majorly messed-up." He could see Nefaria starting to get angry again, so he backed off. "But you can make it better," he assured her. "Set these women free. Let them be themselves again." He could see that his words were having an impact, and he was starting to feel confident that Nefaria would let the women go. He was on a roll! Feeling good about his powers of persuasion, he decided to bring up an even bigger topic. "And when Snow White gets here, maybe you can make up with her, too."

In an instant, the remorse drained from Nefaria's face and was replaced by a newfound rage. "She's coming here?" she asked.

"Oh yeah," Holden said nervously. "I mean, I think. Maybe. But back to these women . . ."

There was no talking to the Queen now. She was full of anger. She wheeled around and began to retreat toward the stairs. "If she's coming here," she sneered, "then I shall be ready for her!" With a wicked cackle, she slammed the door to the dungeon, once again locking Holden and the women inside.

A moment of quiet passed. Nobody knew quite what to say. Finally, Holden sat down, sighing, and began shuffling the cards again. "Like I was saying. This is called 'Slap the 7s' . . ."

Chapter 18

As Maddie and the dwarfs emerged from the dark woods unharmed, Maddie beamed with pride. "We rock, you guys," she said. "Look, there's the castle!" She pointed up the hill, and all seven dwarfs gazed in wonder at the towering palace looming above the valley.

"Ooh! Ahh!" they marveled.

Prince Charming scratched his head. "Just one question. Where's the door?"

"The door?" Maddie gazed at the castle, but to her amazement, she couldn't see a door anywhere.

"Yeah, how do we get in?" Abe asked.

"There must be an entrance!" Bud continued.

"Surely, there's an opening!" Cal insisted.

"Okay, I get it," Maddie replied. She didn't need to hear all seven of them chime in on the topic. "I live here, so of course I know where to find the door. It's right—" She craned her neck, trying to look around the side of the castle.

"Right . . ." No matter which way she looked, she couldn't see any door. Just as she was about to admit she didn't know where else to look, a dark portal opened at the base of the building. "Right there!" Maddie pointed. "I knew it," she added, relieved.

As all of them watched in wonder, the portal grew larger, and a dark silhouette appeared to emerge through it.

"Whoa!" Abe said.

"Magic!" Bud added.

"Someone's coming!" Cal replied.

"Maybe a royal guard!" Don guessed.

"Probably to greet us!" Edd hoped.

"How exciting!" Fox chirped.

As the figure grew closer and more distinct, Gus shuffled his feet nervously. "But just in case, I'm going to stand back a little bit, no a lot, no all the way back at our cottage, yeah, I'm pretty sure that's—"

"My stepmother!" Maddie gasped, as Queen Nefaria's face fell into full view. The Queen spread out her arms, casting a mighty shadow over them all. Maddie wanted to run and hide, but instead she steeled her resolve. This was the moment they'd been training for.

"You guys!" she said to the dwarfs. "It's go time!"

"Kee-yai!" shouted Abe, leading the charge. One by one, his brothers leapt off their ponies and swarmed on the Queen. Bud karate-chopped her left kneecap. Cal karate-chopped her right kneecap. Don kicked her in her right hip. Edd kicked her in her left hip. Fox vaulted off Gus's back and got her in a chokehold.

"Rwar!" they grunted. "Hoo-bah!" "A-murph!" "Umma-umma!" It was a major melee, like one of those ludicrous wrestling matches Holden loved to watch on TV while spilling nacho crumbs all over the floor.

Nefaria swatted at the dwarfs, mildly annoyed. "Hey!" she whimpered. "What are they doing? This is painful!"

Prince Rodrigo decided the craziness had gone on long enough. "Back off at once!" he commanded, stepping into the fray. He pulled the dwarfs, one after another, away from the Queen.

"You don't understand," Maddie told him. "We need to get her before she gets me!"

Rodrigo looked into Maddie's eyes with great compassion. "Snow White, she's your family. You at least owe her a chance to explain."

"Yes, listen to this man!" Queen Nefaria cooed, as the dwarfs backed off. "He's quite . . . what's the word?"

"Charming," Maddie groaned.

"Snow White," the Queen continued, her voice as soft and harmless as a kitten's purr, "I don't know what that huntsman told you, but I would never harm you, my child."

"I believe the huntsman!" Maddie said defiantly. "He told me everything!"

The Queen bowed her head, sadly. "He's crazy, my dear. I had to lock him in the dungeon. He told me he cut your heart out, but what he gave me was just a mushroom. See for yourself."

The Queen pulled out the flattened mushroom, which still bore her footprint from where she stomped on it.

"That's weird," Abe said.

"He doesn't sound all there," Bud agreed.

"I wouldn't trust him," Cal concurred.

Once again, Maddie cut them off. She had read *Snow White* dozens of times, and she knew the Queen was lying. But how could she ever explain that to her friends? "I can't tell you how I know, but I'm positive she wanted me dead. This is all just an act."

"Please, my dear," Nefaria said. "Come with me inside and let me explain."

Rodrigo and the dwarfs turned toward Maddie to see how she would respond. But before Maddie could reply, another voice emerged from the portal — soft and tired, yet hopeful.

"Snow White?" it said. "Is that really you?" Out stepped the King, tears streaming down his face as he set eyes upon his daughter. "They told me you were—" He couldn't finish his sentence. He was so overcome with emotion. "Oh, my dear! I'm so happy to see you!"

He raced up to his daughter and locked his arms around her, sobbing uncontrollably.

"Hi . . . uh, Dad," Maddie replied. It was an unexpected moment, since she'd never seen or heard anything about the King from the story. Once again, she and Holden had made a major change to a fairy tale. Back when she'd first read the story, she'd wondered how the King had reacted to all the drama in his family, and now here he was, reacting. "I'm fine," she assured him. "It was all . . . just a story."

"She's alive and well, Your Highness," Prince Rodrigo said, shaking the King's hand. "These nice gentlemen made sure she returned to you unharmed." He motioned toward the dwarfs.

"Thank you all!" the King exclaimed. "This is the happiest moment of my life." He stepped back, beaming with joy. "Now all your friends must stay, so we can have a celebration! My daughter, my wife, and I, together again as a family!" He put one arm around Maddie and the other around Queen Nefaria.

Maddie felt incredibly awkward, torn between a father who loved her and a stepmother who wanted to murder her. She was going to need Holden's help to find a way out of this, that's for sure. But how would she get to him when he was in the dungeon? She followed the King and Queen inside, with no idea what to do next.

Chapter 19

The Queen had her servants lay out a magnificent fruit platter for Snow White, the dwarfs, and Prince Rodrigo. There were fresh berries, succulent grapes, juicy melons, almost any type of delicious fruit imaginable. The dwarfs wasted no time diving into the feast, stuffing their faces with everything they saw. Prince Rodrigo carefully selected a wedge of pineapple and bit into it with relish.

"What a marvelous treat," he raved. "Your stepmother is really an excellent hostess."

Maddie shook her head. "I'm telling you. It's an act. She's up to something."

"By feeding you delicious fruit?" Rodrigo took another bite.

Maddie had no response. Queen Nefaria's generosity certainly seemed sincere. Then, out of the corner of her eye, she spotted Bud and Cal, the feuding dwarfs, going at it once again.

"Hey!" Bud shouted. "That's my banana!"

"No, I want it!" Cal said. The two of them tussled over a banana, each refusing to let go.

"Don't make me karate chop you!" Bud warned, swinging his free arm.

"Don't make me kick you!" Cal fired back, wiggling his legs.

All the other dwarfs backed off as the fight escalated. "I'd better step in," Rodrigo said. Once again, he approached the bickering brothers to make peace.

As Maddie watched him try to settle the dwarfs' tempers, Queen Nefaria sauntered up behind her and placed a firm, steady hand on her shoulder.

"Not hungry, dear?" she asked.

"No, not really." Maddie noticed Nefaria's warm expression, and it actually made her relax a bit. Maybe Rodrigo was right. The Queen was trying so hard to be kind. Maybe she should give her a chance.

Queen Nefaria reached into her cloak. "Well, I saved the best piece of fruit just for you."

"Oh," Maddie replied. "That was thoughtful, I guess." She couldn't believe how friendly the Queen was acting.

"Yes," the Queen said. She pulled her bony hand from her cloak, revealing her gift to Snow White. "It's your favorite. A crisp, ripe, shiny new . . . apple!"

When Maddie saw the apple resting in Nefaria's palm, she screamed. "No!" Of course! That was the Queen's plan, just like in the original story. She was going to poison Snow White with an apple!

With a quick flick of her wrist, Maddie swatted the apple away, sending it flying across the room and into the side of Prince Rodrigo's head.

"Ow!" Rodrigo cried, rubbing his skull.

The King rushed over, horrified. "Snow White! Why would you reject your stepmother's gift? You love apples!"

"She's trying to kill me!" Maddie accused, pointing her finger at Queen Nefaria.

The Queen gasped. "Never! I would never harm my beloved stepdaughter!"

"It's just an apple," Rodrigo agreed, trying to calm Maddie. He picked the apple off the floor, brushed it against his cape, and placed it back on the table.

"It's poison!" Maddie shouted. "She's determined to kill me. Ask the huntsman! She told him to murder me because she thinks I'm too pretty!" She saw the King stroking his chin, uncertainly. "You have to believe me!"

The Queen placed her arm around Maddie gently and tried to escort her from the room. "Dear, you must need some rest after the ordeal you've been through. You're saying crazy things."

"I don't know what to believe!" the King admitted, throwing up his hands.

"Then bring the huntsman in here!" Maddie demanded. "He'll back up my story!"

"Come now." The Queen held the apple out to Maddie once more. "Sit down, eat this. It will make you feel better."

"I won't touch that apple!" Maddie shrieked.

"Very well," the King responded. "Bring the huntsman here. We'll find out what really happened in the woods."

The King sent his guards away. Maddie felt relieved. She even flashed a triumphant smirk at the Queen. It was only a matter of time now before the truth came out.

Chapter 20

"Boo-yah!" Holden shouted as he tossed his wild card down on the discard pile. "I'm changing the suit to clubs!" Then he stood up and started to dance, swiveling his hips in his opponents' faces. "Take that!"

Once again, the door flew open. This time, it was the guards who appeared. "Huntsman, you've been summoned!"

"Oh, come on!" Holden whined. "Why do you have to summon me when I'm about to win the game?"

"The King has asked for you at once."

"Okay, fine!" Holden tossed down his cards. "No peeking while I'm gone, ladies!"

When the guards led Holden into the throne room, the King, Maddie, the seven dwarfs, and some handsome dude were all calmly waiting for him.

Queen Nefaria, on the other hand, was pacing nervously back and forth, saying, "I don't see why we'd believe the huntsman. He's a liar. Maybe whatever he says, we should assume the opposite, so if he says I told him to kill Snow White, it means I didn't!"

Holden broke out in a delighted grin. This was the moment he'd been waiting for. The Wicked Queen was going to get what was coming to her at last!

"Huntsman, come before me!" the King uttered.

With his head bowed respectfully, Holden stepped up toward the King. "Yes, Your King-ness, or whatever-your-name-is-ness." He was happy to kiss up to this guy if it meant the Queen would be going down.

"Please, tell me what happened when you took my daughter to the woods."

"Right. Crazy day," Holden said. "First we talked about what a major whack job your wife was. Then, I saw a puffer mushroom, which was pretty cool. Then, Snow White did some boring crafting stuff, and I taught her karate." Holden began to demonstrate his martial arts moves. "I was like, 'Kiai! Hee-yah! Yow-yow-yow!'"

Maddie could see the King was growing impatient. "Just tell him what Queen Nefaria ordered you to do."

"Oh, right," Holden replied. "She told me to kill Snow White."

The dwarfs all gasped, and the King buried his face in his hands. "Say it isn't so!" he moaned.

"Oh, it's so," Holden assured him. "It's very so. Like, seriously, it's *so* so."

Then, shocking everyone in the room, the Queen threw herself at her husband's feet, collapsing in anguish. "It's true!" she confessed, her voice breaking. "I did it! I ordered the huntsman to kill Snow White!"

Again, the dwarfs gasped. "I was not expecting that," Gus said. "She kept saying she would never do something like that, but now she admits she did something exactly like that. In fact, she did that! And that's pretty bad."

"Shh!" Prince Rodrigo hushed him.

The Queen pulled herself up, grabbed the King's hands, and stared directly into his stunned eyes. "I wasn't myself! I was mad with jealousy."

The King shook his head, puzzled. "You were jealous of our daughter?"

The Queen bowed her head. "She's so perfect, and I have so many flaws."

"Do you mean your hair?"

Nefaria gasped. "You . . . you knew?"

"Of course I knew. I never mentioned it because I didn't want you to think it mattered to me."

The Queen began to cry. "I was wrong. Please forgive me!"

The King breathed deeply, unsure what to think. "Oh, Nefaria . . . ," he whispered.

Maddie could see him feeling sorry for his wife. "If you really regret what you did," she asked the Queen, "then why did you try to give me a poison apple?" She pointed at the apple on the table.

"It's not poison!" the Queen plead. "I wouldn't do that!"

"Let me see that!" the King said. The dwarfs passed the apple up to him, and he inspected it closely. "I know my wife's magic, and this apple . . . ," he held it up to the light, examining it like a jeweler would a diamond, ". . . has definitely had a spell put on it!" He set the apple down, then looked at his wife with disappointment. "Oh, Nefaria . . ."

"No," Nefaria begged. "Please . . ."

"Guards! Seize her!" The King pointed at the Queen, enraged. "Take her to the dungeon, immediately! And never let her out!"

The guards grabbed Nefaria and began to march her out of the room. "No! No!" Nefaria wailed.

Maddie and Holden shared a satisfied look. It felt really good to see the Queen exposed like this.

"You did the right thing, dude," Holden assured the King. "Although maybe this dungeon's a little too good for her, but you can work that out later."

While the guards dragged Nefaria into the hall, Maddie fist-bumped her stepbrother. "We did it!" she whispered. "That's one more fairy tale fixed, thanks to us!"

"We rock at this," Holden smiled proudly.

"Yeah, I wonder what's next," Maddie said. "*Rapunzel? The Little Mermaid?* Yes! *The Little Mermaid!* I have some ideas for jazzing up the ending to that!"

Holden sighed, thinking about Resplenda and *der Spiegel.* Maddie had no idea they were just one smash away from never having to go near a fairy tale again.

"You know, when our parents got married," Maddie continued, "I started trying to figure out how many days it would be until we both left for college and I'd never have to see you again."

"Whoa, that's harsh!"

Maddie smiled. "I don't do it anymore. I just forgot about it. I think if it weren't for these fairy tales, I never would have gotten used to having you around. I know you may not like these stories, but you're really good at fixing them."

Holden blushed. "*We're* good. We're kind of a team." He thought about his dad's offer to move to Germany, and for the first time, he wondered how Maddie would feel. He knew it would make his mom sad if he left, but was it possible his annoying stepsister would miss him, too?

Behind them, Bud and Cal were at it again, karate chopping each other over something typically petty.

"Take back what you said!" Bud wailed.

"Not until you take back what you did!" Cal screeched.

Holden rolled his eyes. "Geez, what's with those two?"

Maddie shrugged. "They're always fighting."

"How annoying!" Holden said. They watched as Prince Rodrigo stepped in to break the dwarfs apart. "Hey, who's that guy anyway?"

"Oh, that's Prince Charming."

"Well! Smoochy, smoochy!" Holden made kissy faces in the air.

"Stop it!" Maddie blushed. "Snow White barely knows him. Maybe they're not even supposed to be together."

"Well, you should probably try to find out while we're still in the story," Holden said.

Maddie smiled. "I wonder if that's why we haven't been sent home yet."

"Maybe, but I think there's one thing I need to take care of, too."

Now that the dwarfs were calmed down, Prince Rodrigo approached and shook Holden's hand. "It took real courage to stand up to the Queen, Sir." He bowed down to Holden. "If you'd like a fresh start, you're welcome to join me in my kingdom. I could use a new huntsman. And I promise there will be no murders."

"Wow, you are charming!" Holden said.

"Pardon?" Rodrigo laughed.

"Why don't you talk to my sist–" He stopped himself, looking at Maddie. "I mean, my . . . Snow White. I have something I need to do."

Holden backed away, and Prince Rodrigo turned to Maddie, holding his hand out to her. "May I?" he asked.

"Okay!" Maddie replied. She looked down at his hand, unsure exactly what she was supposed to do with it. His palm was up, so she took her best guess and slapped him five.

Rodrigo laughed at her strange response. "You are a funny one!"

Oops, Maddie thought. She realized now she was supposed to take his hand and hold it. Oh, well. She had made a charming man laugh. That had to count for something, too. Rodrigo motioned for Maddie to follow him, and she walked beside him out of the room and into the palace garden.

Chapter 21

The Royal Garden was everything Maddie loved about fairy tales. It was brilliantly bright and colorful. Adorable animals frolicked and played amid the lush greenery. Best of all, she got to share it with a man who was like a piece of art himself — not just handsome, but with inviting, soulful eyes that gazed kindly into hers and a soft smile that welcomed her to gaze back at him. He was a good man, and she could tell he would make Snow White very happy.

Rodrigo led Maddie to an arched wooden bridge over a calmly bubbling stream, and from there, they took in the full beauty of their surroundings. With his head bowed, Rodrigo spoke quietly but firmly. "Allow me to apologize," he said.

"Apologize?" Maddie was confused. What could this sweet man have to apologize for?

"Perhaps I shouldn't have pushed you to make peace with your stepmother. I didn't quite realize how treacherous she was." Maddie had to think back to her vocabulary lessons to remember that *treacherous* meant wicked and untrustworthy. Prince Charming was also Prince Well-Spoken.

It was hard to be mad at this guy, of course. "Don't apologize for that," Maddie replied. "You have a good heart. I only wish she did, too. I actually started to believe for a second that she changed, and I kind of liked the idea of her getting along with Snow White." Maddie caught herself. "I mean, with me. It would've been a nice ending."

"Ending?" the Prince repeated, confused.

"I mean, it would've been a new beginning."

"You're amazing," Prince Rodrigo replied. "To stand up to such a murderous villain . . . I don't think I've ever met anyone as brave as you."

"Brave?" Maddie had to hold herself back from laughing again. Her? Brave? She screamed whenever she saw a spider. She wouldn't go near the high diving board. She still used a nightlight to sleep. She'd never thought of herself as brave.

Then again, she did just stand up to a would-be killer. And the wolves! She fought off a pack of wolves using karate, and she didn't even know karate. That was pretty brave.

Maybe being in these fairy tales had changed her, made her stronger and more mature. She wanted to tell the Prince all the reasons she wasn't brave, but instead, she did something even braver — she accepted his compliment. "Thanks."

Maddie then caught her reflection in the stream and remembered she still had horrible bedhead and morning face. She was amazed that Rodrigo didn't seem to mind her odd appearance, and she felt like it was time he saw her real face. "This isn't what I usually look like," she confessed. She wiped the oatmeal off her skin with her hands, then tried to straighten her hair by running her fingers through it. But that only spread the oatmeal through her hair, which now looked even worse. "Oh, no. Yuck. You don't have a hairbrush, do you?"

Prince Charming chuckled. "It's okay," he said. "No matter how you make yourself look, your true beauty always shines through."

"Awww . . . ," Maddie said, flattered.

"I have to go back to my kingdom," he told her. "I'm needed there."

"Oh, sure," Maddie said, thinking this was his way of saying goodbye. "That's fine. I get it. Well, this was fun."

Prince Rodrigo turned and looked into her eyes, taking her hands in his gently. She couldn't believe a man was holding her hands! And it was Prince Charming, no less! "I do so enjoy spending time with you. I really hope I can see you again."

Maddie took a deep breath. She always wondered how she would handle herself when a boy made it clear that he liked her.

She knew the smart thing to do was to play it cool. She should say something polite but not overly enthusiastic. Something that made it clear she was interested, but didn't make her look desperate for a boyfriend. She thought long and hard, then opened her mouth to reply.

"Eeeeeeee!" she squealed. "You bet you can see me again!"

Well, so much for playing it cool.

Holden marched into the Queen's chambers and right up to the magic mirror with determination. "All right, *Spiegel*. Let's do this." He unfastened his boot and got ready to swing it toward the glass.

"Wait!" Resplenda shouted, appearing suddenly in the mirror.

Holden groaned. "What now? We got the Queen sent to the dungeon. Snow White met her man. Can I please just smash the mirror already and go home?"

"Home?" Resplenda winked. "Sure, you can go home, but which home?"

"What?" Holden asked, annoyed. "What do you mean which home?"

"Well, well, lower your voice. It's time for the snotface to make a choice." Resplenda's face faded from the mirror, and in its place, two separate images appeared. One was his father blazing down the Autobahn on his motorcycle. The other was his mom and Greg, asleep in front of the television.

"Oh, right," Holden said. He had been so busy with the fairy tale that he'd forgotten he had the biggest decision of his life to make. Could he really leave his mom and go live with his dad in Germany?

He put the boot back on his foot, sighing. He needed to think about this for a minute. "I don't know what I want," he confessed.

"I think you do! True, true, true! But just in case, here's another clue!"

As Holden continued staring at the mirror, another person appeared. It was Maddie, in her pajamas, coming downstairs to find their parents asleep on the couch. Very quietly, she turned off the TV and the lights and nudged them both to get them to go up to bed.

Holden looked back and forth between that image and the one of his dad, his heart heavy with the decision, when suddenly, Resplenda reappeared, her face taking up the entire mirror. "Boo!" she shouted.

Holden stumbled backward in surprise, shrieking, "Eesh!"

This cracked the fairy up. "Hee-ha-hoo! I scared you!"

"That's it," Holden said, ripping his boot off again. "This is going to feel so good!"

"Good for you, but not you-know-who!" Resplenda faded, and in her place appeared an image of Maddie holding hands with Prince Charming in the palace garden. "A curse for you is her dream come true!"

Holden felt bad for his stepsister. She loved these fairy tales. She was going to be crushed when she found out there wouldn't be any more visits to these stories. He couldn't believe he actually cared about how she felt. What had happened to him? Was he becoming . . . nice?

He shuddered at the thought, but he had to admit, spending time with Maddie wasn't as horrible as he used to think. He never would've done it willingly, but thanks to Resplenda's curse, he'd gotten to know her better than he ever thought he would. She was actually kind of cool — a little bit — sometimes, anyway. Shattering the mirror would put an end to that, and they'd probably go back to the way they were. Barely even acquaintances, let alone siblings, as distant as could be, whether he lived in Germany or on the other side of her bedroom wall.

"Tell me one more thing," Holden said to Resplenda. "Is Maddie right about the apple? Did the Queen poison it?"

"Ah . . . easy to believe, easy to doubt. If you want to know, check this out!" Resplenda faded from the mirror, and there appeared an image of Queen Nefaria from earlier that day. In it, she picked out the apple she would later give to Snow White. She held it in front of her face, her eyes began to glow, then she said some magic words and a dark mist circled around the fruit. It sunk through the apple's skin as the Queen looked on with an evil smile.

"Maddie was right!" Holden said. He began to back out of the room, when Resplenda's face returned to the mirror.

"There is a curse, I do advise you," she said, "but the one she placed may just surprise you!"

Holden thought about asking her what she meant, but by then, he was already out the door. He couldn't wait to find Maddie and tell her the news.

Chapter
22

Holden raced through the palace, eager to tell Maddie what Resplenda showed him. The apple was cursed for sure. But he couldn't help thinking about what Resplenda said as he was leaving. The curse "might surprise" him? What did that mean?

On his way to the palace garden to see his stepsister, he passed by the throne room, where something very unusual seemed to be happening. His first sign that something strange was going on was the sound of joyful chuckling coming from the hallway. Wasn't this where they just had a woman sentenced to the dungeon for attempted murder? What was there to laugh about?

Holden decided to peek in, and he saw the two dwarfs who were always fighting, only this time, they weren't fighting.

They were hugging. Hugging and laughing and saying the nicest things about each other.

"Aw, you're the best brother!" one of them gushed, with complete sincerity.

"No, you're the best brother!" the other one cheered in response.

"I'm sorry I ever fought with you!" the first one said.

"Well, I'm super sorry!"

"I'm super duper sorry!"

"I'm sorry times infinity!"

"I'm sorry times infinity plus one!"

Holden couldn't believe what he was seeing. They were suddenly getting along abnormally well, and that peacemaking Prince was nowhere in sight. He had to find out what happened, so he walked up to one of the other dwarfs and tapped him on the shoulder.

"Yo. Why are they so lovey all of a sudden?"

"Isn't it brotherly?" the dwarf responded. "They always fought like brothers, and now they're getting along like brothers, because they are brothers, and oh brother! I've been waiting for this moment!"

Holden rolled his eyes. Clearly, he picked the wrong dwarf to talk to. This guy never shut up! He decided to ask one of the other little guys instead.

"What made them make up with each other?"

"It started after they ate that apple," the dwarf replied. He pointed to a shiny red fruit with two bites taken out of it.

"That's the poison apple!" Holden cried.

The dwarf shrugged. "Well, they were fighting over it, and they each took a bite. And then they stopped fighting."

"Huh?" It was so strange. Wasn't the poison supposed to make them fall asleep? Unless this had something to do with what Resplenda said. The curse would surprise him.

Suddenly, Holden figured it out. "It wasn't poisoned! She put a forgiveness spell on it. She wanted Snow White to forgive her!"

Holden took the apple and ran out to the courtyard. He found himself in a mellow paradise, all delicate plants and soft breezes. It was like one of those calming videos with the tinkly music his mom sometimes watched while she was doing yoga.

Across the garden, he spotted Maddie and Prince Charming standing together on a bridge. "Hey, Maddie!" he shouted, as loud as he could. "Yo!"

Every creature in the area bristled at the sound of Holden's barbaric yelp. Birds flocked to the skies. Skittish butterflies sought refuge under mushrooms. Squirrels' fur stood up on end. The calm of the courtyard was shattered in an instant . . . except for Maddie and the Prince. Holden's intrusion didn't even register with them. They kept talking and smiling, just as they had been, so lost in each other's eyes that they didn't hear Holden at all.

"Gross!" Holden commented, under his breath.

He began to run over to them. He'd probably have to pry them apart to get their attention. But just as he approached the bridge, he saw Prince Rodrigo do something unexpected.

He leaned down and put his face close to Maddie's. Oh, yuck! They were going to kiss! Holden wanted to shout again, to dive in between them, anything to stop this moment from happening.

Instead, he decided he would merely cover his eyes and turn his head. He wanted no part of any fairy tale smoochy-smoochy, but he knew this was what Maddie lived for, and he figured just this once, he'd let her have it.

He ducked into some bushes to hide, then wondered how long he would have to stay there before the kissing would be over. How long did people usually kiss for? Two seconds?

Chapter 23

Once Holden explained everything he'd learned about the Queen and the apple, Maddie agreed they should go see Nefaria immediately. Along the way, the dwarfs invited themselves to tag along, in case any karate became necessary. Together, they all descended the stairs to the dungeon. With each step they went down, the lights grew dimmer, the air got colder, and everyone's breath became heavier. Rodrigo stepped to the front of the group, nobly. "Whatever awaits us in there, I'll protect you," he assured them.

Holden rolled his eyes. "Guys, chill," he said. "This place is a party."

Maddie and Rodrigo shared a puzzled look, as Holden confidently pushed the door open. To Maddie's amazement, the room was bright and welcoming. She saw a table full of food and plenty of comfortable places to sit. She almost began to smile, until she heard the sound of deep, pained sobbing.

It took her a moment to discover the source of the tears. It was Queen Nefaria, no longer stern and fearful as she had always been. She was crying openly and holding the hand of a woman with very dirty skin. "Oh, Gracie. What did I do to you?"

"You took my life away from me," Gracie replied, sadly.

"What's going on?" Maddie whispered to Holden, as she tried to make sense of the odd scene.

Holden was already stuffing his face with appetizers from the buffet. "Just sit back and enjoy the show," he told his stepsister.

The Queen winced, turning toward the next woman. "And Lily! You always had such wonderful hair. Sakiya, you didn't deserve this!" She stood up and approached another woman, whose face was covered with wrinkles. "Vivian, I feel like I hurt you most of all. You were my best friend!"

By now, Maddie had figured it out. "So Snow White wasn't the only woman the Wicked Queen was jealous of?" she whispered.

"Duh," Holden groaned.

Queen Nefaria took a deep breath and paced before the prisoners. "I am so ashamed. I cared more about my looks than anything else, and I hurt so many good people. Now, I realize that beauty fades, and only love can last forever. But I don't expect any of you to love me. No one could ever love someone like me!"

Vivian, the wrinkled woman, stepped forward. "I still love you."

"Whoa!" Maddie whispered to Holden, as they watched the scene unfold. "I didn't see that coming."

Vivian placed her hand delicately on Nefaria's arm. "I remember the girl I first came to know as a child, who was so kind and such a good friend to me. I saw how cruel your family was and how much it hurt you. I watched you change as we grew up, until you became someone I didn't recognize. But if my friend is still in there, then I'm willing to give her another chance."

She hugged the Queen, who began crying harder. "You're not just a friend," Nefaria told her. "You're my family!"

The other women were so moved that they all joined in for a group hug.

As Holden watched the women reconcile, he thought about the choice his dad gave him. This fairy tale was wrapping up, and soon he'd be back in his real life. He needed to choose where he wanted to live it.

Maddie sensed he was deep in thought, so she poked him gently to see what was on his mind. "What's up?"

Ordinarily, Holden might've told her to mind her own business, but after all he'd just witnessed with Queen Nefaria, he decided it was better to just be honest. "I have kind of a big decision to make," he said. "My dad asked me to move in with him."

Maddie's jaw dropped. "In Germany?"

Holden nodded. "It's really cool there. And I love my dad. But—" He looked at Maddie, and all he could do was shrug.

"Wow, that is a big decision," Maddie said. In some ways, it was exactly what she'd been hoping for, a chance to get Holden out of her hair for good. But now that it might actually happen, she found herself hoping he would choose to stay.

Across the room, the group hug finally came to an end, and the Queen addressed the other women. "Thank you all, but if I'm going to change, I need to be honest about who I am. There's a side of me you've never seen. The real me."

The Queen lifted her hands to her head and gently pulled off her crown. Along with it came the wig she always wore, revealing the perfectly smooth, hairless scalp underneath.

The women all gasped, as did Maddie and Rodrigo. Everyone was shocked, except of course, for Holden.

"Eh, seen it," he bragged, a little too loudly. "I'm over it!"

Startled, the Queen turned around and noticed the spectators for the first time. "Snow White!" she shuddered.

"Hi," Maddie replied.

"How much of that did you hear?" Nefaria asked.

"Enough to know that maybe you're not totally wicked." Maddie was overcome with emotion herself. "Maybe there is some love in your heart."

"Oh, my darling!" Nefaria said softly. "Is it possible? Is there a chance you could forgive me, too?"

Maddie smiled at her. "You don't need a magic apple to get people to forgive you. You just need to show them your heart."

"So you know about my apple?"

"My brothers ate it," Abe said.

"I love this guy!" Bud continued, pointing to Cal.

"And I love this guy!" Cal agreed, pointing to Bud.

"And we're family!" Don cheered.

"And family is love!" Edd nodded.

"And love is all that matters!" Fox agreed.

Everyone turned toward Gus, as he took a deep breath, gearing up to speak. "Yeah," he said. And that was it.

Maddie stared at him, shocked. "That's all you have to say?"

Gus shrugged. "Well, they kind of said it all."

Maddie smiled at the Queen. "Let's start over again. Having a stepmom can be pretty cool when you get along with her."

"Oh, nothing would delight me more!" Queen Nefaria said, hugging Maddie tightly.

Rodrigo wiped a tear from his cheek. "I love happy endings," he sniffled.

"Oh, come on, dude," Holden admonished him. "This is so sappy!"

The Queen emerged from the hug just long enough to ask Snow White, "Do you think you can summon your father for me? I can only hope he's as forgiving as his daughter."

Before Maddie could reply, a voice called out from the staircase. "He is," it said. The King stepped into the room.

He, too, was quivering with emotion. He dashed into the room and joined the hug. "I just want my family back!" he blubbered.

At this point, Holden couldn't hold back anymore. He was clearly tearing up.

"A-ha!" Rodrigo said, noticing his watery eyes. "Even the huntsman is moved at last!"

Holden hid his face. "Leave me alone!" he whimpered. "I miss my mom!"

The King approached the women who had been held prisoner by his wife. "All of you are hereby freed from the dungeon. You shall be reunited with your families at once. And to make up for the way you've been treated, a feast will be held in your honor!"

While everyone celebrated, Maddie walked over to her stepbrother, smiling. "I guess everyone, even the wickedest villain, deserves a second chance," she said. She didn't realize it, but as she spoke these words, she had already begun to fade from the scene. Their work in this fairy tale was done.

Chapter
24

The next thing Maddie knew, she was staring at the back of the Wicked Queen's head, at what was clearly a wig. She could see her speaking to her magic mirror and getting angrier and angrier.

"Snow White!" a man's voice called out. Maddie looked over and saw a familiar man holding a clipboard and wearing a headset. "You're almost on!" he told her.

The Wicked Queen turned and walked past Maddie. As she did, she softly whispered, "Break a leg!" That's when Maddie realized it wasn't Queen Nefaria. It was Tasha, in her costume for the play. The auditorium was packed, the spotlight was shining, and the show had just begun. It was time for Maddie's entrance.

"That's your cue!" the stagehand told Maddie, giving her a nudge. For a moment, Maddie was gripped by stage fright. She and Holden had just changed everything about this story. How would she know what to say?

Thankfully, as she stepped onto the boards, every line became crystal clear in her mind. She knew them not because she had memorized them from a script. She had actually lived them. Crafting a heart from a mushroom, karate chopping at a pack of wolves, even a first kiss with Prince Charming. (The way they staged it, she and Jake Templeton turned away from the crowd, so the audience couldn't see they were merely kissing on the cheek. You wouldn't know it was anything less than a romantic smooch, though, from the way the audience whooped in excitement — and the way Maddie blushed as Jake leaned in.)

Eventually, the play came to an end just the way the story did, with Snow White, the Queen, and the King sharing a group hug, while the dwarfs and the women in the dungeon looked on. "All of you are hereby freed from the dungeon," said the King, played by a boy from Maddie's science class. "You shall be reunited with your families at once. And to make up for the way you've been treated, a feast will be held in your honor!"

Then the spotlight turned to Maddie, and everyone waited for her to say the line that would close the show. It took her only a moment to realize that the words she needed to say were right on the tip of her tongue. "I guess everyone," she said, projecting confidently to the very back of the auditorium, "even the wickedest villain, deserves a second chance."

As soon as she said it, the audience leapt to its feet and a roar went up from the crowd. The curtain fell, and Tasha high-fived her friend. "We did it!" she said. "You were awesome!"

The cast quickly scrambled backstage, taking their places for curtain calls. Maddie watched as they stepped out, row by row, to take their bows. Tasha earned squeals of approval, but it was nothing compared to the love people showed Maddie when she curtseyed to the audience. Her dad stepped forward and handed her the most beautiful bouquet of flowers she had ever seen, even prettier than the ones in the castle's garden.

She could tell it was a moment she would treasure for the rest of her life. Somehow, though, something seemed missing. One face was absent from the crowd, and right now, it was all she could think about.

Maddie did her best to have fun at the cast party, but it wasn't easy. Her mind kept straying to Holden and the big decision he had to make. Would she ever have to hear his crummy music again? Or have him embarrass her at school? Would she have to share her next birthday with him, or would she have her special day all to herself again?

Throughout the night, Maddie's friends all complimented her on her performance. They insisted she re-create the scene where she scared the wolves away with her crazy karate. It was everyone's favorite.

At the end of the night, Maddie called her dad, and he told her it was okay to sleep over at Tasha's. The two girls stayed up late, and after everyone else had left, Tasha sat down to talk to her friend.

"You know you killed it in the show, right?" she said. "Why do you seem so mopey?"

Maddie couldn't hide her feelings anymore. She decided to tell her what was going on. "I just found out that Holden might be moving to Germany," she said.

"Awesome!" Tasha shouted. "That's the best news ever!" She saw from Maddie's expression that she wasn't quite as excited. "I mean, isn't it?"

"I don't know," Maddie said. "I kind of got used to the little weasel."

The next morning, Maddie's dad came over to pick her up. He asked her if she had fun, and all she could muster was a half-hearted, "Yeah."

"What's wrong, honey?"

Maddie shrugged. "Just thinking about Holden."

Her dad pulled around the corner onto their block. "Well, in that case, I have some bad news for you."

Maddie's breath stopped for a moment. "Bad news?"

She looked ahead to their driveway, where Carol's car was pulling in just in front of them. "He beat us home," her dad said with wink.

"What?!" Maddie watched in shock as Holden stepped out of his mom's car with his suitcase. As soon as her dad parked, she threw open the car door and jumped out to face him. "You're back? For good?"

"Eh, I got tired of bratwurst," he replied.

Maddie rolled her eyes.

"I mean, my dad's awesome. But I wanted to stay with the rest of my family."

Carol turned her car off and stepped out, smiling. "He called me last night while you were at the party. He said he wanted to surprise you."

Maddie smiled. Holden snapped his fingers in disappointment. "Aw, I was hoping you'd cry when you saw me! 'Boo hoo! He's back!'"

Again, Maddie rolled her eyes. She was closer to crying than he realized, but not because she was sad.

"Come on, you guys," Maddie's dad said, stretching his arms out wide. "Family hug!"

Greg, Carol, and Maddie came together in an instant, embracing each other warmly. Holden groaned, but soon, he joined in, too, mostly to get it over with. Maddie thought back to the group hug at the end of Snow White, when the whole family, despite their differences, came together as one.

In that moment, Holden knew he had made the right decision — not just to come back to Middle Grove, New Jersey, but to leave Snow White without smashing the mirror.

Maybe he'd get to fix another fairy tale. It wasn't such a bad job, and somebody needed to do it. The stories were definitely a lot better with all the hoverboarding and karate fights he added. He was providing a valuable service, even if Maddie got to have her input along the way, too.

Maddie, of course, didn't know how close Holden had come to breaking their spell. As she wrapped her arms around Holden and her parents, she was already dreaming of the next time she and Holden might get to travel into one of her favorite stories. She couldn't wait. The fun, the danger, the romance — it was all so incredibly magical to experience.

Even if she had to share it with her rotten stepbrother, who maybe wasn't so bad after all.

THE END

About the Author

Jerry Mahoney loves books — reading them, writing them, and especially ruining them. He has written for and ruined television shows, newspapers, magazines, and the Internet. He is excited to finally be ruining something as beloved as a fairy tale. He lives in Los Angeles with his husband, Drew, and their very silly children.

About the Illustrator

Aleksei Bitskoff is an Estonian-born British illustrator. He earned a master's degree in illustration from Camberwell College of Arts in London. In 2012 he was a finalist for the Children's Choice Book Award. Aleksei lives in London with his wife and their young son.

Glossary

acquaintance (uh-KWAYN-tuhns)—someone you have met, but do not know very well

admonish (ad-MAH-nish)—to scold someone sternly

concur (kuhn-KUR)—to agree

guillotine (GIL-uh-teen)—a large machine with a heavy blade, used to cut off the heads of criminals

melee (MAH-lay)—a confused fight or scuffle

mutilate (MYOO-tuh-late)—to injure or damage something or someone by spoiling its appearance

petty (PET-ee)—small and unimportant; mean and spiteful

robust (roh-BUHST)—strong and healthy; powerfully built

siege (seej)—to attack someone or something violently

taunt (tawnt)—to try to make someone angry or upset by saying unkind things about him or her

visualize (VIZH-oo-uh-lize)—to imagine something; to see something in your mind

Think Again

1. How do you think a real-life master of karate would react if he or she saw Maddie's moves? Just for fun, try writing a scene where Maddie takes her first karate class.

2. Holden can't believe that Queen Nefaria has a magic mirror that can answer any question, yet all she ever asks is whether anyone is more beautiful than she is. What else do you think Nefaria should ask her mirror? They can be serious questions like "How can you get someone to forgive you?" or silly questions like "What's the best way to defend yourself against a karate-chopping dwarf?" What questions would you ask a magic mirror?

3. At around the same time Maddie decides the Wicked Queen deserves a second chance, she realizes she should give Holden one, too. Can you think of other ways Holden has been a villain to Maddie, in this book or in the other books in the series? Why do you think she changes her mind and decides at the end that he "maybe wasn't so bad after all?" What do you think Maddie and Holden's relationship will be like after the book ends?

Let's Talk About Ruining Dialogue

Dialogue is a fancy word for characters talking to each other. It can be one of the hardest things for a writer to write, but once you get the hang of it, it's also probably the most fun. The trick is to make sure your characters sound different from each other. Think about the people you know. They don't all talk the same, do they? Listen to how your best friend talks. Then, listen to your grandma. I bet they sound nothing alike, right? (Unless your best friend *is* your grandma, of course, in which case, she's one lucky lady!) When you start to notice the differences in the way people talk, you're on your way to writing great dialogue.

The key is to start with interesting characters. I love writing Holden because he always says what he's thinking, and unlike most people, he doesn't care if something comes out sounding not so nice.

Resplenda's dialogue is fun to write, too, because it's so unusual. Since she's a fairy, she doesn't have to talk the way real people talk, and that allowed me to come up with my own rules for the way she speaks. She loves to talk in rhyme, for one thing. Plus, she has a bunch of her own sayings, like "Yodely-ho!" and "Toodle-oodle-oodle" and "Magica magica bing bang zow!" Things you'd probably sound silly saying to your parents or your teacher. I always look forward to writing Resplenda's scenes, because I know I'll get to put in some kooky dialogue.

Here's an exercise to flex your dialogue-writing muscles. Try writing two very different characters. One can be a kid about your age. You can even model him or her after someone you know. Then, make the other character an imaginary creature. Maybe it's a fairy like Resplenda, or a mermaid, a talking unicorn, a goblin, a genie, a robot, a ghost, a zombie, a witch, an alien. Anyone who would have a fun, unique way of speaking. Use your imagination!

Now, write a conversation where the kid wants something that the creature doesn't want to give him or her. Maybe a girl tries to hire a mermaid to give her swimming lessons, but the mermaid is running late for a water polo game. Or a boy attempts to convince a goblin not to eat him, but the goblin hasn't eaten in three days, and there's nothing he finds yummier than little boys with brown hair. Imagine what that conversation would sound like and how the two of them might eventually work out a solution.

And have fun — because if you're having fun writing the dialogue, then people will have fun reading it, too!

Jerry

FIND MORE MAGICAL STORIES AT
WWW.MYCAPSTONE.COM

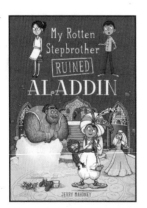

My Rotten Stepbrother RUINED **ALADDIN**

JERRY MAHONEY

My Rotten Stepbrother RUINED **BEAUTY AND THE BEAST**

JERRY MAHONEY

My Rotten Stepbrother RUINED **CINDERELLA**

JERRY MAHONEY